FOR THE BETTER

A PREQUEL TO LEFT TO YOU

DANIEL J. VOLPE

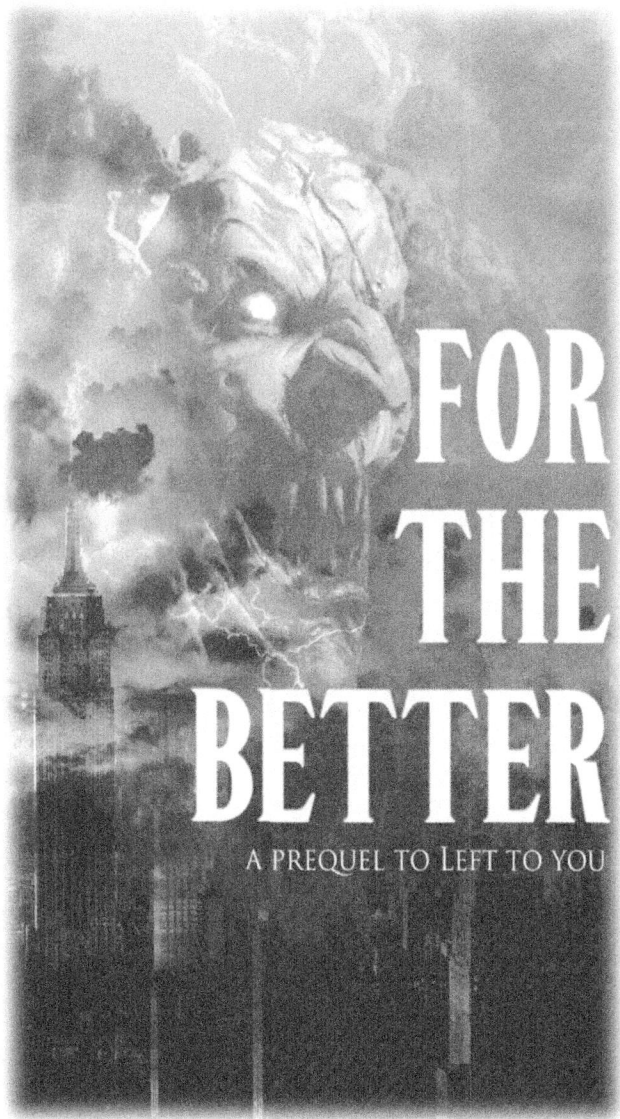

FOR THE BETTER

A PREQUEL TO LEFT TO YOU

COPYRIGHT

Edited by Mary Danner

Cover art by Don Noble

Interior layout by Matt Wildasin.

Copyright © 2024 Daniel J. Volpe.

ISBN: 978-1-961758-15-5

MORE WORKS FROM
DANIEL J. VOLPE

Billy Silver

Awakened In Blood

Talia

Talia 2

Only Psychos

A Gift of Death

Black Hearts and Red Teeth

Sew Sorry (w/ Aron Beauregard)

Plastic Monsters

A Story of Sorrow books 1-3

Multiple Stab Wounds

Through The Eyes of Desperation: The
Black Version

TO THE SURVIVORS

PREQUEL? MORE LIKE A MID-QUEL

STOP!!!!

If you haven't read *Left to You*, don't read any further and go grab that. This isn't a marketing ploy, but an actual warning.

Okay, did you read it? Good, now you may continue with this foreword.

When I first set out writing *Left to You*, the story just seemed to flow. It followed a natural progression, breaking itself into numerous parts. But there was always one part I felt was missing. How did Josef live for decades with the demon, Belphegor, in captivity? What did he do to keep himself younger so that in *Left to You,* he's nearing 120 years old?

While writing *Left to You,* I kept asking myself these questions, but it just didn't feel right at the time. The story already jumps between a few timelines, and the last thing I wanted to do was add a whole bunch more. So, for the sake of the readers' sanity, I skipped over that part. Just know that Josef used the demon's powers to keep himself healthy, okay?

Nah, that wouldn't fly for me either. I just had to know. Who or what did Josef sacrifice to keep himself in good health? Were they people, animals, a combo of both? And if he did kill people, who did he kill? I don't feel like Josef was an evil character, but he was definitely a survivor. That was quite evident with his time in Auschwitz, and the lengths he went to make it out of the camps. As desperate as he was to be reunited with his family in death, Josef fought to survive.

I think Josef's turning point, at least in my eyes, was when he made the decision to kill Kollmer in New York. It was one of the first times we actually saw him exhibit hatred and follow through with it. While in the camps, he had a brief thought about killing Private Berg, knowing he could overpower the demur Nazi, but out of self-preservation, he didn't act upon it. Once free and again given the opportunity to kill one of the death-dealers, Josef acted. Those actions set into motion a chain of events that changed not only his life, but the lives of many others.

So, this book isn't quite a prequel, nor a sequel, it's a midquel. It picks up right after Josef kills Kollmer and is left with Belphegor in his control. This book covers Josef's life with the demon, how he coped with loss and grief, and the lengths he went through to survive.

I always thought Josef was one of my purest characters, but after writing this book, I'm not so sure.

FOR THE BETTER

Chapter 1- 1952

The glow of the cigarette was the only light in the dark room. It quivered, dancing between Josef's nervous lips.

He took a drag and held it in his lungs for as long as he dared. His pulse pounded as the smoke begged to be released. Slowly, he let it slither from his mouth. A glass of bourbon sat on the end table next to his pack of cigarettes. Josef picked it up and sipped. His vision wavered. He was on the verge of being drunker than ever before. It was what he needed. There was no way in hell sleep would come for him, not that night. He feared it might not return for some time.

"The motherfucker did it," Josef said. He finished the bourbon in his glass and refilled it. Drinking from the bottle would've made more sense, but he couldn't bring himself to do it. After all, he wasn't a drunk, not yet anyway. The amber liquid sloshed in and out of the glass, wetting the table. Josef took a gulp, letting the fierce bourbon burn his throat.

Burn like the fires of Hell.

Josef hated Nazis. He hated every one of them, with Lieutenant Kollmer being one for the ages. But when Josef watched the demon rip the man apart, a human flicker of sympathy flashed for just a moment. Only for a moment, and then it was gone like ash in the sky; like the ash of the millions of corpses incinerated at the death camps. Josef flicked his cigarette into the ashtray, looking at the pile of gray in there. During his fateful stay at Auschwitz, he'd seen many people turned to ash, burned in the massive ovens meant for human flesh. He saw them falling from the sky, wafting like black snowflakes, akin to those his sons used to catch on their tongues.

That was behind him, at least physically. His mind, however, would never leave the camp. His body left when he escaped war-torn Europe for America. He thought he was leaving it all behind, but the day he saw Kollmer, he knew differently.

The man saved him during his imprisonment, but he was the last face many Jews saw before death, a smiling face that took great joy in ending life, savoring the fear of the condemned. Josef hated him, and yet, knew he owed him his life.

It didn't matter anymore. Josef went to Kollmer's store with murder on his mind. The man may have saved him, but his crimes could never be forgiven.

Josef, for his entire life, would never forget the last time he saw Kollmer alive. The man, the fucking sick, twisted piece of human garbage, had captured a demon. Not just any demon, but a prince of Hell. He'd trapped Belphegor.

When Josef saw the monstrosity in the store's basement, he couldn't believe it. The stench of burned matches and shit made his eyes water, but he had other, more human, monsters to slay.

FOR THE BETTER

Pushing Kollmer towards the demon had been one of the worst and best moments of his life. It sickened him to think that way, but for every squeal and scream Kollmer made, Josef remembered a face. The face of a young child murdered in the gas chambers. An old woman shot in the head because she couldn't work. Millions of others whose screams went unheard as the Nazis laughed before pulling the trigger. Killing Kollmer was the right thing to do, but it left Josef with a problem. A major problem.

What was he supposed to do with a demon?

I can help you. Feed me and let me help you.

The demon's voice was in his brain, calling to him. It was insidious, burrowing its way into his subconscious. Josef didn't think he'd ever sleep again, not after watching the monster rip apart a human and consume his flesh.

Josef stubbed the cigarette out in the ashtray, lit another, and finished his drink, which he didn't need. What was done was done. He rose on wobbly legs and stumbled to his tiny bedroom. The only thing he did was kick off his shoes before crawling into bed. Sleep wasn't going to come quickly, considering what he'd seen only hours earlier.

He set the burning cigarette in the ashtray he kept next to his bed, something Ola would've never allowed. Looking up at the spinning ceiling, he did his best to push the gruesome death from his mind. He just wanted to rest, to seek a reprieve in the dreamland of his mind. The room spun like he was in a tornado as his eyes steadily grew heavier and heavier.

A trail of smoke from the smoldering cigarette rose into the darkness above. It melted into the gloom. Watching its rise helped Josef focus.

So familiar, he thought. His eyelids drooped, staying shut for a moment longer than normal. *It looks like a chimney; a happy chimney attached to a fireplace.* He smiled, but it was short-lived. *No, it fucking doesn't. It's not a happy chimney, it's an evil chimney. It's not a chimney at all. It's a fucking smokestack.* His eyes stayed closed even longer. Voices from the past began chattering in his ear. *I've seen that before. I've loaded it...with the dead.* His eyes closed and his breathing slowed. *It's where they burned them: my family—my wife and boys.* Sleep took Josef, but it would not be restful. No, it would be Hell, pure fucking Hell.

Josef was in Kollmer's office again. It was commonplace for him, which was a blessing and a curse. His eyes were locked on the ground like he was in trouble, and he couldn't raise them at all. Not even a little. They were focused on the wooden floor of the room and his worn shoes.

"So," a rough voice said, "what should we talk about today?"

Josef's head was released. It snapped up like it was on a spring. He expected to see Kollmer sitting smugly at his desk with a plate of food and a pitcher of water. The evil Nazi was gone, replaced by something worse. Much worse.

Belphegor sat nude in Kollmer's chair. Twisted horns rose from his head. Black eyes were sunken deeply into his face. His mouth was a nightmare, bristling with sharp teeth. Bugs crawled over him, seeking pus-weeping holes littered amongst his flesh. In front of him lay a plate, but what it contained was not food; at least, not for any normal human being. On the plate were piles of shit, wet entrails, rotten meat, and human fetuses.

"Oh, where are my manners?" the demon growled. His Hell-born face split into a grin and he offered the plate to Josef with a flourish of his clawed hand. "Will you eat?"

A burp rose in Josef's throat. He stifled it with the back of his hand, but his throat burned with stomach acid. Rather than speak, he waved, refusing the plate.

"That's a damn shame," Belphegor said. He pulled the plate back in front of him. "A drink then?" The demon lifted a pitcher from the desk—the same one Kollmer used to keep full of clean water.

Josef's throat was dry, and he desperately needed something to wash away the sting of bile, but he knew better. Again, he refused the offer.

"Fine," Belphegor said.

The pitcher was a slurry of putrescence. Chunky vomit, blood, liquid shit, and God knows what else came sliding out of the pitcher. A cup overflowed with the mixture, spreading on the desk.

The demon ate.

Juices poured from Belphegor's mouth as he crammed his maw with every morsel on the plate. The slurry ran down his nude chest, mixing with pus dripping from his open wounds. With the meal finished, he upended the cup down his throat, then looked at Josef and belched.

Josef's stomach clenched at the offensive odor.

"Delicious, but I still have a hunger. I hunger for something a little," he put a clawed finger in the air and twirled it, "fresher."

On cue, the office door opened. Private Berg came walking in, looking nearly pristine. Josef didn't notice anything different about the man until he saw the back of his head. Wet bone and brain matter glistened under the office lights, highlighting the exit wound of the self-inflicted gunshot.

"Yes, sir," Berg said.

"Bring them," Belphegor, who still had his eyes on Josef, ordered.

Berg nodded and backed out of the office.

"Papa!" Piotr and Michal screamed as they were led into the room.

Josef's head snapped, watching his two sons escorted into the office in the hands of the Nazi Private. "Boys," Josef yelled. He tried to stand, but couldn't. It was as if his body was cemented to the chair. Even his arms were locked tight.

16

"Oh Josef, you're alive," Ola wept as she was ushered in behind her sons.

The trio stood off to the side of the desk, weeping and looking at Josef.

"Leave," Belphegor ordered.

Berg snapped a crisp salute and closed the door behind him.

Josef was crying. He couldn't believe they were alive and looking so good. They looked well fed and their clothing wasn't filthy; it was as if they'd just walked off the train.

"Do you love them, Josef?" the demon asked with a sneer.

Josef didn't want to take his attention from his family, fearing they'd disappear like an apparition—like dandelion fluff in the wind. "Yes, more than anything," he cried. His head involuntarily turned to face the demon. He struggled, straining his neck, but was powerless, and did his best to keep them in the corner of his eye.

"I can help them. Free them from this hell and set you free. Would you like that, Josef?" Belphegor smiled again. His hands were in front of him, creating a tent.

Josef's mind raced. That was the easiest question ever. He didn't care who it was, or how they helped, as long as his family was safe. If given the chance, he'd switch places with them in a heartbeat. "No, fuck them," Josef said to his horror. A phantom voice, one sounding like his own, came from his throat like a speaker box.

The look of shock on his face must've been hilarious because the demon slammed the desk in laughter. "No? Really? I thought you said you loved them?" Belphegor asked.

If he could've raised his hands, Josef would've used them to cover his mouth. *Yes! Fucking yes! Help them, you bastard!* He wanted to scream. "I don't need them," Josef said. "Ola is a cunt, and these fucking brats were a mistake, a night of drunken sex that should've never happened."

The cries of his family cut Josef deeply. Tears ran down his face as he tried to fight his tongue, but he couldn't.

"Papa," one of the boys—Piotr, he believed—cried, "you don't love us?"

Slowly, Josef's head turned back to his family.

They all wept; Ola had a look of hurt scorn on her face and both boys cried openly.

"I pictured this going differently," Belphegor said. "Well, their fate is sealed, but yours—I guess I should say *ours*—is still open for interpretation. I can give you anything, Josef, as long as you bring me meat."

A horrid stench invaded the room, worse than when Belphegor was eating.

"Watch, Josef. Watch your family. See their fates. See what your cowardice did to them. You wanted to stay behind and try to wait out the war instead of fleeing. Your mistake did this."

The room erupted in screams.

FOR THE BETTER

His family was nude, as if their clothing had never existed. Ola screamed as blood poured from her vagina. Josef heard the scraping of tools, the cutting of blades, and the laughter of Nazi doctors who weren't there.

"Ola!" he screamed, his voice was back under his control, but he still couldn't move his head or close his eyes to the torment. "Let them go, please! I'll give you whatever you want. Just help them!"

Belphegor laughed. "They are gone, Josef. Ash on the fucking wind, but their souls are with my brothers. And they know pain; yes, they do."

His sons' high-pitched screams were painful, boring into his eardrums. Both boys shivered in their nudity as the torture they'd suffered manifested itself on their little bodies. Their eyes turned different shades as toxic dyes were injected. The skin on their chests opened under unseen knives. And their screams…

Josef's eyes blurred as tears streaked down his face. "No, no, no," he muttered, but couldn't look away as his sons were dissected in front of his eyes.

The burning smell got stronger and Ola's feet started smoking. The flames started at her toes, hissing as they evaporated her uterine blood. Yet, she wasn't dead. "Josef, fuck you!" she screamed as the flames crawled higher.

"Papa, why?" Piotr, whose face was a carved mess, asked. His legs were ablaze. The smoke of his flesh obscured his torso.

Even in the smoke, Josef could see his son's wet organs.

"Papa, please, make this stop," Michal begged. He, too, was ablaze.

The acrid smoke burned his nostrils and stung his eyes as he watched them be immolated.

"This chapter is over, Josef, but our story is just beginning. Bring me meat and I can give you everything," Belphegor said.

Josef screamed as the room filled with smoke, and then, he was burning…

Josef jumped up, pulling himself out of the dream. His chest still burned. He looked down at the smoldering cigarette. "Fuck," he said, swatting away the butt.

The cigarette flew to the floor, and he stamped it out. It had burned through his shirt and left an angry red blister. He thought he'd put his last smoke out, but clearly, he was mistaken.

He sat on the edge of the bed with his head in his hands. The pain of the nightmare corrupted his mind like oil on water. It clung to him, washing him in grief. Each passing second brought another hellish moment to the forefront of his mind.

His pack of cigarettes was nearby, and he grabbed one. For a moment, he considered going to get more alcohol, but thought better of it. His head was spinning and the last thing he needed was to drink more.

Early morning light was starting to pinken the sky. He stood and went to the window. The silhouette of Manhattan was black against the sky in the distance. The city that never sleeps. Josef felt like the man who never sleeps. He took a drag of the cigarette and let out the smoke; the sting of it hitting his eyes brought him back to the nightmare.

The demon—Belphegor—was out there sealed in a rock, in the basement of a store owned by a Nazi. It was all too surreal. Maybe Josef died in the camp and this was his Hell? No, it was real.

Outside, in the rumbling of early traffic, he heard a dog bark. The city was full of strays running wild in the streets, killing rats, and knocking over garbage cans.

Josef remembered Kollmer's dog, the one he'd stepped on when he attacked the man. The dog was still in the apartment, probably scared and wondering where its master was.

"Fuck," he said as he stubbed out the cigarette and rubbed his face. He needed a shower and something to eat. Once he felt human again, he'd go back to the city and get the dog, facing the demons of his past.

Josef expected Kollmer's apartment to have a few cops crawling around, but there were none. The store was locked tight, and Josef still had Kollmer's keyring in his pocket. He tried not to look suspicious, but Josef didn't think that was possible, not that anyone paid him any mind.

The city was waking in full. Even early, the streets were full of cars, buses, and human traffic. People on their way to work, performing the countless jobs which kept the bustling metropolis afloat.

Josef walked up the stairs to Kollmer's apartment, looking over his shoulder as he did. He didn't know what he expected. Maybe the cops would grab him, or Belphegor possibly escaped and was waiting for him. Neither happened as Josef shuffled through the keys.

Kollmer's dog barked on the opposite side of the door. Its little nails scratch against the wood with excitement.

Josef opened the door and the little dog jumped on him. It paused when it realized he wasn't its master, but dogs were simple creatures. A few good rubs and a calm voice and they were best of friends.

"Schatzi," Josef read the tag hanging from the dog's collar.

The dog's ears perked up at hearing its name.

"Let's get you something to eat and get the hell out of here."

Schatzi wagged her tail and licked his hand.

CHAPTER 2

It had been two days since his encounter with Kollmer, and yet, his body still hadn't recovered. Sleep was a distant memory, and the few fleeting hours he got were full of nightmares.

Josef sat at his small desk in the office he shared with another professor. A stack of papers desperately needing to be graded mocked him. The swirling text danced on the page in front of him, shifting with every glance. His eyelids were heavy and, slowly, they closed. He snapped awake when his head slipped from his hand.

The cup of coffee next to him was cold, but he picked it up and sipped anyway. Coffee in America had taken some getting used to, but like other things, he grew to like the bitter blend. At least it was *real* coffee and not the horrid concoction served to him in the death camp.

With a little caffeine in his veins, Josef rubbed his face and picked up his red pencil, ready to read.

...in Freud's work, he touches on subtle nuances of ripping your wife's tits off and fucking her to death. And then, I'll force-feed your sons my rotten shit until they fucking die...

Josef blinked. His heart was thudding as he picked up the paper, pulling it closer to his face. Nothing. No evil text, just another bland report about Sigmund Freud.

The office door was ajar and it swung open on squealing hinges.

"Sorry," Eryk said as he walked into the cramped office.

Josef looked up at him, happy for the interruption. He put the paper down. "No problem at all." He grabbed his coffee and winced at the coldness. "I needed the distraction."

Eryk squeezed past Josef. He had a stack of papers in his arms as well. He settled in at his desk. "Too much reading makes my brain hurt, that's for sure." Eryk took his jacket off and hung it on the back of his chair.

"Yeah, that…" Josef looked up at his colleague. "…amongst other things."

Eryk donned his reading glasses and was prepared to dive into his work when he stopped, looked up at Josef, and slid the glasses off.

"Nightmares?"

Josef licked his lips, tasting ash. He touched them and smelled his finger before licking his lips again. Nothing. "Yes, nightmares. But they keep getting more and more real. Like I can't wake from them."

Eryk nodded towards the open door, which was almost directly behind Josef.

Josef stood and closed it.

"For years I had the same problem, but my stay in the hellish camps wasn't nearly as long as yours."

FOR THE BETTER

Eryk had been one of the lucky ones, if that was even possible. He'd always been one step ahead of the Nazis, running from their death squads. The thought of fleeing to America, or anywhere else for that matter, seemed like an impossibility, and to him, was almost pointless. The *Blitzkrieg* was bulldozing Europe and Africa, and it was only a matter of time before the world fell, at least in Eryk's eyes.

He was a single man. His parents died in a car crash years before the war, he'd never married—women weren't quite his thing—and had only a few close friends. It was much easier for a single man to get lost in the war than it was for a family. Finally, Eryk was caught and narrowly escaped death because of his wit and strength. Like Josef, he was tasked with manual labor, but his work wasn't loading corpses. His tasks were more menial, such as digging, or even some manufacturing work. Still, he saw his share of horrors, horrors which followed him to the New World when he could finally run.

"What did you do with the nightmares?" Josef asked.

Eryk pulled a thermos from a drawer. He set it on the desk and unscrewed the top; the smell of fresh coffee filled the room as steam rose from the opening. "Top off?" he asked, holding the metal container aloft.

"Please," Josef said, and offered his mug to Eryk. With his cup almost full, he reached into his desk, removing a small bottle of bourbon. "Top off?" he asked, a pained smile on his face.

Eryk hesitated and nodded. "Yes, I think this conversation calls for it."

Josef dumped a generous amount in their cups.

Both men sipped in silence, contemplating their thoughts.

"What did I do?" Eryk asked. He cleared a spot on his desk and set the cup down. "At first, nothing. I suffered in silence, letting myself be held hostage by the memories." His eyes wandered to a spot on the wall, his face going blank. Eryk blinked and shook his head, trying to shake something from his vision. "But I knew that wasn't the way. I couldn't go on like that, waking in fear every night, screaming at the visions of black boots and Death's Head pins. But who was I supposed to talk to, huh? Other survivors? Should I dump my problems on them when they may have been able to heal their wounds?"

My problems might be a little different, a bit more complex, Josef thought. *Not every survivor has killed their tormentor, only to find out he had captured a demon, which was now their responsibility.* He sipped and listened.

"So, I kept a record of them, every one. Each nightmare I had—awake or asleep—I'd jot it down. And you know what? They began to slow. The intensity would be dull, at best, and I could always control them. It was like getting the poison out of my body, but through a pen." Eryk sipped and grimaced at the amount of liquor in his cup.

26

"That's it? You just wrote and it helped you?" Josef asked.

"Well...yeah, I guess. But again, this might not help you, or anyone for that matter. But for me, it was a Godsend." Eryk opened his desk drawer and rooted around. "Here, take this."

Josef reached over and grabbed the leather-bound journal from Eryk's hand. The black cover was soft and welcoming. "Thank you." He turned the book over and thumbed through the blank pages.

Eryk waved him off and sipped again. "Ah, my pleasure. I bought that as a backup, in case I had a nightmare here, but sometimes these kids are enough of a nightmare to make days in the camp seem like a breeze."

Both men knew that was a lie, but shared a laugh anyway. It felt good to laugh, to be normal for a moment in time. Just two men, who'd suffered greatly, joking about the worst time in human history.

Josef walked into his apartment to the sound of little paws rushing towards him.

Schatzi came running up, jumping for his attention.

"Okay, okay," Josef said. He set his briefcase down and tossed his jacket onto the chair before crouching to greet his new dog.

He petted Schatzi, and she quickly rolled over, offering her belly to him. Days earlier, when he stepped on the little dog before murdering her former master, had all been forgotten.

They went into the tiny kitchen. There, he dumped a scoop of food into her bowl and gave her water.

He sat at the table smoking a cigarette and thinking. Kollmer was dead, but more problems had arisen. Josef felt no guilt about killing the man, even if it involved feeding him to a demon. It was a proper, and deserved, death. His concern was the store and what secrets lie underneath.

Kollmer had money, but there were always bills to be paid. Whether it was rent, utilities, or anything else, people would start looking for their money, and the first place they'd go was to the store. It might take some time for the bank to seize the building, but when that day came, what would become of the stone? Would the hellish altar be taken as an eccentric man's work and boxed up and sold, or would someone recognize it?

Josef was at a loss. He knew he could take the stone and book, but the thought of going anywhere near it made his skin crawl. Something had to be done, and it couldn't be done from his kitchen table. He stubbed out his cigarette just as Schatzi finished her dinner.

The little dog sat at his feet, tail wagging.

He couldn't do anything from his apartment. He had to go back to Kollmer's. "Come on, girl.

We're going on a little trip." Josef rose, Schatzi at his feet.

She began barking with joy as he grabbed her leash.

It was getting dark earlier and earlier. A chill was in the air, and soon, the snow would come.

Josef walked with Schatzi down the street, his jacket closed around his neck. He felt bad for the little dog, but she didn't seem to mind. Every so often she'd stop to squat, but other than that, she was happy to be out and about.

He shivered, not from the cold, but from seeing the store in the distance. Part of him wanted to be inside the apartment, if only to escape the chill. But another part of him dreaded the trip. He felt like he lost a piece of himself every time he made the journey.

Kollmer's apartment was just as he'd left it. It was obvious a scuffle had happened. Josef made a note to straighten up before he left. He didn't think anyone was stopping in soon, but it was better to cover his tracks.

Schatzi, recognizing her former home, began running around, searching, but her previous master was nowhere to be found.

Josef began searching, too, starting with the desk in the living area.

Kollmer was, not shockingly, a very organized man. Papers were filed and labeled in cabinets, account numbers were documented. It was all right in the living room/office area, but Josef had an itch. An itch to search further.

A closed door at the end of the hallway beckoned to him. It called out as if it had a voice. It wanted him to enter, to snoop around, to find its hidden treasures.

Josef stood, almost automatically. A flash of his dream burst into his brain, of when he'd lost control in Kollmer's office. Well, in the nightmare, it was Belphegor's office. Each step forward felt like an intrusion. He knew what he was going to find would be the end of him. It was like tearing the scab from a wound that was almost healed and pouring salt into it. Nothing good could come from entering Kollmer's room, yet he walked.

He twisted the cold doorknob and the door swung open soundlessly on well-oiled hinges. It smelled stale and unlived in, but there was a presence about it, like the den of a wolf. The room was unadorned and devoid of Nazi memorabilia.

Josef didn't know what he expected; that he would open the door and it would have a swastika painted on the wall in blood? Or Kollmer's SS uniform would be hanging on a mannequin ready to be worn?

The room was simple, with a small bed and tasteful art on the walls. A dresser and a tiny nightstand were the only other furniture in the room.

A book—theology-related, of course—and a pair of reading glasses rested on the nightstand.

Josef calmed slightly, but still felt uneasy.

Even Schatzi hadn't followed him into the room; she knew something evil had once lurked there.

Maybe it still did.

A military footlocker sat at the end of the bed, covered in a heavy quilt. Josef pulled the quilt, exposing the locked trunk. He tugged on the lock, but it held fast.

The keyring.

He grabbed the keys from his pocket and began shuffling through them. It took a few tries, but eventually, he found the right one. Josef took a deep breath and threw open the lid. Clothes and more books, but that was it.

"No, there's no way the evil just left him," Josef said. He began pulling books and stacks of clothing from the trunk, tossing them onto the bed.

Kollmer was a smart man, that was for sure. Keeping memorabilia of the past, of the atrocities he and others committed, would be a death sentence. After the Nuremberg trials, many Nazi sympathizers, and Nazis themselves, went deep underground, fearful of facing the hangman. If anyone deserved death, it was Kollmer, and the fate he'd received was much worse than a long drop with a short rope.

The trunk was empty, down to the wood bottom, but he saw something odd: on the side was a notch. It was small, almost unnoticeable, but Josef's keen eyes saw it.

"What the fuck?" he muttered. Josef picked at the notch with his fingernail, but couldn't find purchase.

He walked out to the kitchen and grabbed a knife from the drawer.

Schatzi emerged from her hiding spot, tail wagging, but quickly fled when Josef went back to the room.

The blade fit perfectly in the notch, and Josef pulled.

A false bottom, he thought. The wood moved and shuddered, begging to be lifted. Josef pulled, creating enough of a gap to get his fingers underneath.

Horror awaited him.

The false bottom wasn't very large, just enough to conceal the treachery that was Lieutenant Kollmer. Shiny SS and Death's Head pins glimmered against a backdrop of black felt. The black hat of the SS death squad was piled atop a folded uniform.

Josef pictured Kollmer locking the doors and donning his uniform, presenting himself in the mirror for inspection from a higher-up that would never come. His boots would be shined, reflecting his soulless face. Buttons would be at a high polish, and his face clean-shaven.

Touching the uniform sickened him, but he moved it out of the way. Books and photo albums were buried even lower. Josef touched the covers of the albums. Vomit bubbled into his throat, and he fought not to spew into the trunk. He picked up the first one and opened it.

Pictures of the past stared at Josef like a slap in the face. The first few pages were disturbing, but not because they contained atrocities. No, they contained pictures of Nazis, some of the most evil human beings to exist, acting like normal people. They were joking, laughing, playing cards, and even swimming. It was like looking at an album from some of his college students on holiday. The men and women in these pictures had committed some of the most horrific war crimes in history, and yet, they were able to enjoy themselves like it was nothing to play a game of backgammon in the evening, only to usher women and children into gas chambers in the morning.

Josef flipped through the album. Then, the pictures grew worse. Much worse.

Piles of corpses stacked high.

The walls of the gas chamber etched with desperate claw marks of the victims trying to escape the sweet-smelling death of Zyklon-B.

Men weeping as they kneeled before mass graves, with grinning Nazis at their backs with pistols in hand.

Josef slammed the book shut and could swear he smelled the almond stink of Zyklon-B in the pages. He threw the items back in the trunk and re-locked it. The room suddenly felt small. Sweat soaked his armpits and crotch and he staggered with his first step. Another wet burp rose in his throat, and he knew it wasn't staying down.

He burst through a door in the hallway, hoping it was the bathroom, and collapsed in front of the toilet and purged himself.

Schatzi came running up to see what was going on and stood at the doorway watching Josef wretch into the bowl.

He rinsed his mouth in the sink and flushed the toilet. "I'm okay, girl," Josef said to the dog.

Schatzi sat wagging her tail, her tongue lolling out of her mouth. She stood and did a quick spin, letting him know she was ready to go.

Josef was calming down, but the images lived on in his brain. He grabbed a pad of Kollmer's personalized stationery and his checkbook from the desk and left, hoping never to return.

The nightmares were back: his family being ripped apart, the horrors of death, the things he'd done to survive, Abe...and the dogs.

Josef sat up in bed, sweating. He turned on the lamp next to the bed and grabbed his cigarettes. The flame from his lighter danced in front of his eyes, but he didn't quite see it. He was focused on something else.

The leather-bound journal rested next to his bed.

FOR THE BETTER

Lighting his cigarette, he picked up the blank book. It felt good in his hands, like it was meant for him. He rifled through the pages and an urge came over him, an urge to write, to pour himself into them. Josef opened his nightstand drawer and found a pencil. He adjusted his pillows and sat up, resting the book on his knees.

With Schatzi at his feet, Josef wrote.

18th, October 1952

I have never done a thing like this and don't know if it will become a habit, but sleep is a fickle bitch and likes to evade me. When the Sandman does come, he brings gifts of nightmares and terror. So, this, this diary, journal, whatever it shall be deemed, is my attempt at saving a shred of my sanity.

I write this entry from a place of guilt. A deep, black well of despair that I've never faced in all of my years. I've lost everything: my old life, my family, my identity, and I fear, my sanity. And yet, I'm alive and reasonably healthy. Yes, the joints ache from time to time and my stomach is softer and rounder, but I'm here. They, my wife, Ola, and twin boys, Piotr and Michal, are not.

They are gone, dead in the worst way. Killed in a death camp for no reason besides our faith. We put our faith in a God that could not save us, not even in our darkest hour. Sure, we prayed to him, begged him for forgiveness, to pluck us from the misery that was Auschwitz, but our prayers, and the prayers of millions, went unanswered. And this God, this great being, found it appropriate to let me live. I escaped fairly unscathed, rescued by the Red Army at the end of the war. Even when I was sure death had come for me in the form of a bullet, I was saved.

Why? Why spare me when all I want is to see my family in the Kingdom of Heaven? To feel the touch of my Ola and to lift my boys, smiling at their laughter. This too was taken from me. Death was taken from me. Many times I've thought about ending it, stepping in front of a train or bus, but I couldn't do it. I'm not afraid of dying, but I fear not seeing them again. If I take my life, I may be barred from seeing them in Heaven.

Then again, I am now a murderer. Although, it could be argued that I killed dozens of men by alerting Kollmer about the assault in the camp. Those deaths, even though they were a matter of survival, live on in my soul. They stain me, slick and greasy like a bad cut of meat. The screams from the gravel pits and the knowledge of their true purpose will haunt me.

But what about Kollmer? I killed him. I murdered him, feeding him to the demon he summoned, a demon that was brought forth by the pain and suffering of men, women, and children. A monster pulled into our realm by my doing, allowing an evil man to become something of nightmares.

I don't know how to feel about killing Kollmer. The man was pure evil, but he was also the only reason I survived. Granted, he used me, allowing my knowledge to aid him in his nefarious ways. His death was bittersweet. The world was rid of an evil man, but now something worse has taken his place.

Belphegor, a prince of Hell.

Even writing that feels evil. The name bespeaks hatred and greed—an evil unlike any other. I see him in my dreams. He haunts me nightly, tempting me, teasing me, and snatching it away like a wisp of crematorium smoke on the breeze.

But is he real? This question has plagued me since the day I slammed shut that basement door. Is the demon real, or am I going insane? The logistics of it are absurd. On one hand, I tell myself it was a figment of my damaged mind, that I killed Kollmer in the basement, beating him to death and locking his rotting corpse in his mausoleum. Then again, I'm a rational man and believe what I see. My eyes have never deceived me, and even in my traumatic state, I feel the monster is real.

If Belphegor is truly locked in a stone and at my beck and call, what then? Could he help me like he claims? Was it his hellish powers that allowed Kollmer to escape the dragnets of the Allies and get him to the US unscathed? Or was that just coincidence and luck? I know I don't want to find out. If anything, Faust has shown what making deals with the devil can lead to. My soul may be damned already, but I will not punish myself any further.

My eyes are burning as I write this. The sun is rising on another day in New York, with the majestic skyline in the near distance. Never in my life

DANIEL J. VOLPE

would I have believed man could create such massive buildings, but they did it. I am going to attempt to sleep again, if only for a few hours, but something is better than nothing. I know the nightmares will come, as I've expected them to. And with them will be hope, dashed away in the worst ways possible. And screams will float on a breeze smelling like almonds and death.

God, I wish I'd died with them.

CHAPTER 3

The city streets ran gray with the last remnants of winter. Piles of snow were long gone; only the most stubborn lumps of ice remained on the sidewalks and dark alleys. For Josef, it was like awakening from a long, fitful slumber.

As a boy, he enjoyed the winters in Poland, but he grew to detest them. His joints had begun to ache over the years, and the back-breaking work of the camps left his body worn. Even though it had been years since his liberation, he was still paying the toll for the torment suffered at the hands of the Nazis, physical and emotional.

Winter also pulled him back to the camp. Life there was tough to begin with, but the winters were the absolute worst. Many prisoners died, frozen and malnourished, in their beds. To keep warm, prisoners would huddle together, often prompting severe repercussions from Nazi guards. Warm blood would steam on the cold ground after a bullet would find flesh. The others would scatter, leaving the man to die alone.

The cold was fleeing, making way for spring, the season of new chances and rebirth.

Josef had the radio turned low in the background as he cleaned up his breakfast. Golden sunshine flooded his apartment—Schatzi found herself a nice patch of sun to rest in. Josef hummed with the music as he finished putting away the last few dishes. Eating for one involved little cleanup.

A small pile of paper sat at his kitchen table. Josef lit a cigarette and grabbed a pen. He opened Kollmer's checkbook and began writing.

Since leaving his apartment and store, Josef knew something had to be done with the property. If it was left unattended, it might raise some eyebrows, but wouldn't cause too big of an issue. Now, if it was left unpaid, that would be a problem. Josef didn't mind the bank seizing Kollmer's assets for non-payment, but he couldn't let the stone and book disappear. That was something he'd need time to consider. A talisman containing such power and responsibility couldn't just be left to anyone.

After examining Kollmer's handwriting, and practicing, Josef forged a letter to the bank, advising he would be out of the country for an extended period. All mail regarding his business was to be forwarded to Josef's address, and monthly checks would still be mailed. And Josef did just that. Every month, he filled out a check and sent it in on Kollmer's behalf.

Josef sealed the envelope and looked down.

Schatzi left her place in the sunlight and stood at his feet. Her little tail was wagging as she looked up at him, pacing.

"Okay," Josef said. "Let's go for a walk."

The little dog yipped in excitement and ran to the door where her leash hung.

FOR THE BETTER

Josef put on a coat and slid the envelope into his pocket.

The streets in Yonkers weren't nearly as busy as those in Manhattan. Still, the early morning crowd was just as eager to get where they were headed.

Josef and Schatzi walked, her name tag jingling like a bell on her neck as she pranced next to him.

The day was shaping up to be a nice one, and since Josef didn't have to work, he was thinking about how he and his dog would spend the rest of it.

Josef felt tension on the leash and figured Schatzi was relieving herself. He turned and looked, prepared to clean her poop, when his heart sank.

Schatzi had collapsed. Her body flopped and shook like she was touching a live wire. Her eyelids fluttered and the whites of her eyes were the only thing visible.

"Schatzi!" Josef shouted. He crouched down, unsure what needed to be done.

The dog's bladder voided, spreading a puddle of urine onto the sidewalk. Finally, after what felt like an eternity, the shaking stopped, but Josef knew something was wrong with his dog.

Tears stung his eyes as he picked her up. She was wet with urine, but Josef didn't even notice as he walked down the street looking for help.

"I'm sorry, Mr. Lazerowitz, but there's not much more I can do for her," Doctor Fields said. The elderly vet washed his hands and dried them on a towel next to the sink, then sat on a stool and opened Schatzi's file.

Josef wept. He rubbed the little dog, who was resting after a dose of medication.

She looked up at him with dull life in her eyes. There was pain there, but also love, something Josef hadn't seen or felt in years.

When he took Schatzi from Kollmer's apartment, he had no desire to keep the little dog. He planned on bringing her to the nearest shelter after the first night, but when she greeted him in the morning, he decided to give her a shot. The next day, he found her sleeping next to him, comfortable in bed, with not a care in the world. Josef knew he couldn't get rid of her. It wasn't her fault she was originally owned by a monster. Not any longer; her life would change for the better, and she'd live out her days loved by Josef.

Unfortunately, it looked like her days were coming to an end.

"She doesn't appear to be in pain, Mr. Lazerowitz, but sometimes dogs have good pain tolerance and hide it well. I can perform the euthanasia if you'd like. If not, I'll send you home with medication, which should keep her comfortable, until…" he didn't finish, there was no need to.

Josef sobbed and leaned over the table. He covered Schatzi with his arms, holding her. In her weakened state, she still found the energy to wag her tail. Her pink tongue flicked out and licked his face, giving him the okay to let her go. With a flutter of her heart and thump of her tail, she told Josef, 'Thank you for the love and friendship, and that it was her time.'

She would be okay on the other side, but would Josef be okay without her?

Dr. Fields stood. "I'll give you a moment to decide." He left the room, leaving Josef and Schatzi alone.

The dog's breathing was slow, but her heart still thumped. There was still life in her, Josef knew it.

"I won't let you die here, Schatzi. No, I won't let a stranger poke you in this cold room surrounded by smells of death." It was clinical and clean, but Josef had flashbacks of the camp. His mind raced, thinking of what the offices of Nazi doctors looked like. He doubted they were welcoming or clean, but like them, this office was where things came to die. "No, I won't allow it. You'll come home with me, and I'll keep you comfortable. I'll be with you when you die, I promise." He was nose-to-nose with her.

Schatzi's whiskers tickled him as her nose twitched.

Josef ran his fingers through her fur and kissed her head.

His decision had been made.

Schatzi slept peacefully next to Josef, snoring in the delicate way only a little dog could accomplish.

He wished he could join her, but sleep refused to come to him. Gently, Josef petted her, and she wriggled under his fingers, not waking. Josef stared at her, watching, until finally, his heavy eyelids closed.

The pet shop was full of barking dogs. Josef was hit with the smell of urine and cleaner when he first walked in. The twinkle of the bell over the door sounded as it swung shut behind him. Each wall was full of small cages containing dogs.

He didn't remember walking to the shop, or why he was even there, but he was.

Schatzi was at his feet, excited to be amongst so many other dogs. She barked and yipped with glee, tugging at her leash to see the other animals.

"Easy, girl," Josef said. He crouched down to pet her.

Schatzi jumped up on him, licking his face.

"Should we get you a new friend?"

"Why, a new friend sounds great," a voice said from behind the counter.

Josef's blood ran cold. He knew that voice.

FOR THE BETTER

"We have plenty to choose from here at *Auschwitz and Sons*," Kollmer said. He lifted part of the counter and stepped out. A freshly pressed Nazi uniform—the same one in his trunk—looked like it was just starched and ironed. The Death's Head glistened with evil intent on his hat, and the Luger at his hip looked black and deadly. "We have all kinds of pets, including Jews. Say, would you be interested in a pet Jew, Pet Jew?" He smirked.

Josef stood and backed away, Schatzi growling at his feet.

"Hey now, you don't remember me, old girl?" Kollmer said. "I was your first master. You had a good life with me. Now, you are the pet of someone inferior."

Schatzi still growled and the hair on her back was raised. Her little teeth were bared in anger and hatred.

"Well, it doesn't matter. I'm told you have little time left anyway."

Schatzi's growling slowed, and finally stopped.

Josef looked down at her as a seizure locked her up.

The dog spasmed and writhed, the whites of her eyes flashing behind fluttering eyelids. Liquid shit burst from her in a streak of repulsive red and brown.

Josef fell to cradle his dog.

"Oh, don't fret, Pet Jew, we have plenty of other creatures for you to choose from," Kollmer said.

Josef lifted his head with the sting of tears in his eyes. For the first time, he noticed what was truly in the cages.

Mutations born from Hell lurked behind the steel bars. Children—horrifically mutilated—whined and moaned. Their skin was flayed, and limbs severed. Black stitches wept green pus. Their blind, white eyes were milky and dripping. Scalps were bare, with bloody skulls glistening in the harsh lights of the pet shop.

Other creatures rattled their cages. Dogs with two heads snapped at the bars, mangy mutts, drooling acid from jaws full of yellowed teeth. Flea-bitten mongrels with bare patches of mange, leaking blood.

"These beasts, and many more, await your dear dog—my former baby girl," Kollmer said. "They will fuck her, beat her, and eat her every day. Trust me, I know things, disgusting things, Pet Jew." Kollmer walked closer to Josef, who stood to face him. "But, it can change. She can be better…for a price." Kollmer waved his hand like a magician.

The monsters in the cages disappeared as if they'd never existed. Instead, each of them was filled by identical versions of Schatzi. Happy, healthy versions of the little dog in her death throes at Josef's feet.

"She can live and live long, Pet Jew." Kollmer's voice changed, like he'd swallowed broken glass. "She can live, or she can die and become mine."

Josef looked away from the duplicate versions of his dog and stared into the disgusting face of Belphegor.

The demon wore Kollmer's uniform, which was shredded and torn from his mass. Remnants of the Nazi hat rested on his wooden-like horns, and wet bugs crawled over the buttons.

Abject horror washed over Josef's face at being so close to the monster. He could smell the fetid odor from Belphegor's body. It took every ounce of strength to maintain his gorge as the demon picked a fat, dripping worm from one of his many lesions and ate it.

Black ooze dribbled from the demon's fanged mouth as the bug squished and was consumed. "I can make this happen. I can save her, and you know it. The Nazi told you that and trust me, I can do that, and more. Just bring me meat! Delicious meat." Belphegor took a step forward.

Josef tried to back away, but couldn't. He was frozen, unable to move, just like Schatzi, who was still locked in a seizure on the floor.

"Take me from the stone. Use me for your greed," Belphegor said. He reached out and grasped Josef's shoulder with his clawed hand. "I will save her, but if you let her die…" the demon let it hang in the air. He smiled as green snot ran down his face.

Josef couldn't move. He couldn't even talk, just stood there terrified.

Belphegor's mouth opened wider and wider. His hellish tongue uncoiled like a snake, extending towards Josef's face.

Josef fought, trying to turn his head away, but the tongue kept lurching forward.

Belphegor licked him, leaving behind a trail of slime. The demon kept licking and licking...

Josef awoke with a start as Schatzi licked his face. He caught himself—the dream washing over him like oil—before he accidentally pushed her away.

With his heart in his throat, Josef reached out and petted the dog, who'd become frailer over the past few days. She was the only good thing in his life, and he felt like losing her would send him spiraling into the abyss.

Josef knew what his decision was, but in his mind, he was trying to talk himself out of it. He couldn't sacrifice another living thing to save his dog, could he? What would happen if he summoned the demon and it escaped? Would the city be doomed, or even the world? His fingers played in the dying dog's fur. He tried talking himself out of it, but his mind was made up.

His mind wandered to the stray dog that was always lurking around the shop.

Chapter 4

There was something wrong about being in the shop at night, something deviant, like he was committing a crime. Technically, he was, at least in his mind, what he was doing was something criminal. But it was for the greater good. At least, for *his* greater good.

The stray was a mangy-looking mutt, some kind of shepherd, but with longer hair. The dog looked like death warmed over. It had a face full of scars, patches of fur were missing, and its left eye was cloudy. It was an old scrapper, a fighter on the streets. But even warriors had to eat. When Josef tossed down chunks of stew meat, the old mutt couldn't help himself, and followed Josef right into the back of the shop. Josef set a pile of meat on the floor and grabbed the rope. When the dog's head was lowered, Josef threw a makeshift lasso over its neck. It bit and thrashed, but years of malnutrition and fighting took the battle right out of the animal.

"I'm sorry, little fella," Josef said. He unwrapped more meat and tossed it to the dog.

Not a creature to look the other way for a fresh meal, the mutt devoured the last bits of meat. It licked the floor clean of any leftover blood.

"Come on, old fella," Josef said. He led the dog towards the basement steps. At first, the dog was apprehensive, but Josef was prepared. Another small pack of meat was wrapped in butcher's paper in his

49

pocket. He held it out, just close enough for the dog to smell it. "Atta boy."

The basement smelled normal, but to Josef, the taint in the air the demon had brought forth lingered. It was unclean.

The dog smelled it too, tensing as they walked closer to the steel door under the building. He tensed, but the thought of filling an empty belly was greater than fear.

Josef unlocked the door and entered the room. It looked exactly like it had when he'd last been there, when he killed Kollmer, sending him to a violent, and well-deserved, death.

The dog froze and growled. Josef slammed the door shut and immediately wrapped the length of rope around the knob, shortening it enough so the dog couldn't bite him. Though, Josef didn't think the dog would be attacking any time soon. The old cur pushed his face against the door and cried. Hot piss ran down his leg in pure fear.

Josef looked at the markings on the ground and the candles, and the cages full of animals along the wall. He was sick to his stomach, but the thought of losing Schatzi won out. He knew this was the only way.

The book felt sickly in his hands as he flipped through the pages. It was just to stall himself as he worked up the nerve to complete the ritual to bring forth a prince of Hell into his realm.

The black stone sat unmoving and dripping evil. It was a mark, a blight on humanity, a chunk of stone harboring a depth of evil that few had ever seen.

Some of the animals in the cages were still alive, but many were dead. The stench of their decay was sickly sweet. Josef found a cage with kittens and one of them slowly opened its eyes.

"Sorry, I'm so sorry," he said. Josef opened the cage and removed the kitten.

The cat looked at him with rheumy eyes, too weak to fight. A pathetic meow croaked from its dehydrated throat as Josef's grip tightened around its neck. The small bones snapped with barely a flick of Josef's wrist. He set its corpse in the circle next to the stone.

He grabbed the box of matches and lit the candles, which formed a ring around the stone. With the flickering flames dancing, Josef found the nub of chalk and went over every rune, just as Kollmer had done. They looked good before he'd re-traced them, but he wanted to be sure the ritual was done properly.

Satisfied, Josef left the circle, heading to the pedestal holding the book.

The dog cried hard and scratched at the door, but it held fast.

Josef opened the book and read. The words felt like dirt on his tongue. Something evil and wretched and not of this world, yet, Josef read.

The candles danced as if in a breeze, and the few surviving animals regained some stamina, screaming and shrieking.

Black ooze seeped from the stone, something akin to filth. The blackness rose, taking shape as it did.

Josef had to stop himself from gagging. The stench of the demon was nearly too much for him. A hellish concoction of burning shit and matches filled the air.

The mutt had stopped trying to escape and whimpered alone.

The blackness shifted to crimson, like arterial blood, as it rose higher and higher.

Belphegor stood in front of Josef. The demon, like days before, leapt at the circle, only to be stopped by the wards surrounding it. Belphegor smiled, allowing drool to run from his mouth.

The demon was squat, shorter than a man. Its flesh was covered in boils and sores, each weeping various shades of pus. Insects, bloated and grotesque, waddled out of the demon's many pustules. Belphegor's head was topped with wood-like horns—raw and bloody at the base.

Like in his dreams, Josef watched the demon flex its three-clawed hands.

Belphegor was nude and his penis hung soft and large, nearly touching the concrete. His foreskin was red and angry and acid dripped from his piss slit, hissing as it hit the floor.

"Ah, I see the Nazi taught you well, Pet Jew," the demon hissed, referring to the wards keeping him at bay. "What a shame. I would love to taste your flesh." He looked past Josef at the cowering dog.

"But I see you've brought me a little snack. How wonderful."

Josef stood back from the circle. He didn't even want to be within arm's reach of the monster. "Yes, but only if you help me."

Belphegor smiled. "I knew you'd be back, Pet Jew. You fucking humans are all alike, and they say I'm the greedy one," he huffed. "Greed is the number one virtue of you filth. Greed and lust." Belphegor grabbed his cock and waved it at Josef. "So, what must I do to enjoy this mangy morsel?"

Josef didn't know what to say, but he knew it had better be perfect. He had a feeling the demon would mince words, and this would be for naught; the stray dog's life would end horribly, and Schatzi would still die.

"I want to make a trade. A sacrifice," Josef said.

"Go on," Belphegor replied.

"This dog," Josef pointed back at the stray—he couldn't look at him any more than he had to, "for the health of my dog, Schatzi."

Belphegor rubbed his chin with a claw. Viscous ooze clung to the bone on his hand. He sucked it clean. "Deal, now give 'em here." The demon moved to the edge of the circle. The wards glimmered as Belphegor touched the protection.

I can't do this. Josef thought. *This dog doesn't deserve to die, even though a life on the streets is not much of a life at all.* Josef turned and grabbed the rope. He untied it and tugged at the terrified dog.

"Yes, meat!" Belphegor growled.

The dog, as if realizing it was in trouble, pulled against Josef.

"Come on," Josef said. He yanked the rope, pulling the dog even closer to the barrier.

With its life on the line, the dog attacked.

Josef's leg was on fire where the dog's teeth sunk into his flesh. For a moment, his mind flashed back to Abe, his once-friend who was killed by dogs in the camp. Josef now knew why the man feared the animals.

He punched the dog in the top of the head, once, then twice. The second strike hit the dog in the eye, eliciting a yelp from the mongrel, and it released its jaw.

With his damaged leg, Josef kicked the dog as hard as he could, sending it hurtling towards the circle.

Belphegor waited with outstretched claws.

The dog entered the protective barrier and into the grasp of the demon.

Josef turned away, praying it was over quickly. There was a scream, which was nearly human, and cries of anguish. And then, chewing.

"Delicious. The fear is my favorite part, Pet Jew. Animal fear is so wholesome. They know nothing of life, just survival. And when they're scared, it's genuine," Belphegor said.

Josef turned, afraid of what he'd see. He thought back to the remains of Kollmer, mangled and twisted at the demon's feet.

A pile of bloody fur and shattered bones lay in front of Belphegor.

His mouth was slick with blood and a furry ear was wedged between his teeth. "Bring me human meat, Pet Jew, and I can give you much more than the health of your fucking mutt," Belphegor growled. He picked the ear from his teeth and swallowed it. "There are, what you would consider, 'bad' people everywhere. I care not for their sins, only for their stinking gut and raw marrow. I want to taste their shit as they lose control at my touch. I want to fuck them, stuffing my rotten cock into them, pumping them with my toxins."

Josef couldn't speak. Tears stung his eyes, and with a shaky hand, he grabbed the holy water.

"Human meat, Pet Jew, and I can give you anything. Pussy, money, fame, health, whatever you want."

Josef blocked him out. He tried not to look at the mangled remains of the mutt.

The holy water sizzled as it hit the demon.

Belphegor smiled as he turned into ooze and was trapped back into the stone.

Time seemed to stand still when Josef was with the demon, and the sky was dark when he arrived home.

His keys jingled as he unlocked the door, and a pleasant sound greeted him: barking.

Josef threw the door open, nearly hitting the little dog. "Schatzi girl," he said, and nearly wept as he flipped on a light.

Schatzi danced at his feet, yipping and jumping. She spun in circles as if she'd never been sick. Even her fur, which had gone gray around her muzzle, was dark again. She looked like she was born anew.

Josef hadn't known what to expect when he walked up to his door. Part of him thought he'd committed a terrible atrocity for no reason, making him just as bad as the Nazis. Albeit, killing a dog, even horribly, wasn't as bad as the crimes committed in the death camps.

Seeing Schatzi alive and healthy was a double-edged sword. Of course, he loved her and wanted to see her healthy, but a part of him knew he'd unlocked something evil, something that could be manipulated and used at will. It was a power he didn't want, and yet he had it. Or, it had him.

Josef attached the leash to Schatzi's collar and led her outside into the night air. Overhead, the stars shone bright against the blackness of the sky.

FOR THE BETTER

It has been over a month since my dance with the demon, Belphegor. Schatzi is like a new dog. At first, I thought it was a ruse, something to get my hopes up, only to be dashed to pieces. But, after a month of perfect health, I'm beginning to believe the power of the demon is genuine.

My fear is also genuine.

No, I don't fear that my dog is somehow cursed, although many would beg to differ. She knows no better, only that she went to sleep sick and awoke healthy. I would never claim to know the mind of a dog, but the mind of a human, now that scares me.

I know my mind, my proclivities, and my temptations. I can say with certainty that if I'd had access to this power while in the camp, my life, and that of my family would've been much different. I wouldn't have hesitated in the slightest to push a Nazi, or even one of the prisoners, into the circle where the beast lay in wait. Now, it is different. My family is dead and gone. Even if I begged the monster for their return, I know it could not happen. If it were to come to fruition, what abominations would he produce? Surely, the earthly bodies were gone and their souls in Heaven. In the Kingdom of God, a realm I one day hope to enter.

I am not a greedy man, but I am flesh and blood and not without sin. The demon is on my mind almost daily. When I look at Schatzi, I see the monster. Is her life a blessing or curse? There is evil in this world, that is certain. What if I could use that evil for good? What if I could feed a human monster to the demon, bringing joy into the world? But who am I to play God? Who am I to decide that someone's life should be forfeited just for a glimpse of something better? And who is to say the demon would continue to work? He, being a prince of Hell, isn't known for honesty.

I just know there's a reason this was left to me, but I fear I'll never discover it. I pray for strength, to be strong, and not use this curse for my own selfish needs.

I hope I am strong enough.

CHAPTER 5

Spring rolled into early summer. The cool nights and warm days morphed into sweltering days and uncomfortable nights. Josef and Schatzi slept with a small fan running in the open window, but it did little to relieve them of the heat.

Josef didn't care for the warmth; he still remembered the inferno of the camps. His bunk was sticky and stunk of death. Unwashed bodies covered in corpse-juice were crammed in, raising the temperature to dangerous levels.

That was nothing.

Those who worked at the crematorium had it even worse. For hours, they stood next to the roiling inferno, feeding the flames stacks of emaciated corpses. Men, women, and children were all consumed by the fire.

Josef woke sweating. For once, it was sweat from the heat and not from a horrid nightmare. Over the past few weeks, the nightmares had abated, but not gone away completely. Belphegor and the horrors of Auschwitz still lingered in the back of his subconscious. For as long as he lived, he didn't think those thoughts would leave his mind. They were tattooed on his brain just as his number was on his left forearm.

Josef lumbered into the kitchen and filled a glass with water. He gave Schatzi a fresh bowl as well, but the little dog was distracted.

Her head tilted as they both listened to the footsteps approaching the front door. Schatzi growled as the mail slot on the door swung open. Furiously, she attacked, rushing forward and barking at the enemy—the mailman.

"Quiet," Josef said. He walked over and picked up the small pile of letters that had fallen on the floor. Still half asleep, Josef thumbed through them and stopped. "Oh, shit."

The letter was plain looking, but ominous. A letter from the bank, the bank that owned Kollmer's property, quivered in his hand.

He knew the day would come when he'd have to return to the shop, but just the thought filled him with dread. He hadn't been there since the day he sacrificed the mutt for the life of Schatzi.

The sound of the dying dog haunted him, but when he saw Schatzi happy and healthy, it made it all worth it.

Josef tore open the letter and read.

Dear Mr. Kollmer,

It has come to our attention that utility work will begin in the area of your establishment. New meters are being installed and we would appreciate it if you could provide us with an accurate reading of your current usage. This is crucial to ensure the utility company does not have any unforeseen errors in billing and that all information is carried over properly. Please contact us immediately with these readings at the listed phone number.

Thank you for your time,

Jay Wilburn
Account Director

Josef read the letter over and over. It seemed like a simple task, but was one which needed to be completed promptly. The last thing he wanted was a member of the bank snooping around inside the building. Outside, he didn't mind, but inside could pose a problem.

"Sorry, girl, but I have to run out for a few hours," Josef said.

Schatzi drank and looked up at him. Water dripped from her chin and her tail wagged.

"I won't be long, I hope."

He dressed quickly and left, hoping to catch the next train into Manhattan.

Feeling like a thief, Josef walked into the back of the shop. It was a forbidden place; a lair holding evil, born of evil. But he needed to be there, at least for a few moments.

The shop stunk of staleness. A fine layer of dust covered the collectibles, but Josef didn't care. He wasn't sure what his end game was with

Kollmer's store, but getting the bank off his back was the next step along his winding path.

Josef found the numbers he needed for the bank and jotted them down on a yellowed scrap of paper at the counter. A loud bang made him scratch an errant line across the numbers. "Shit," he muttered.

There was a man at the door. The man had his hands cupped in front of his face and was peering in. He waved and when Josef didn't wave back, he banged on the glass, harder that time. It was hard enough to make the small bell above the door jingle.

"Sorry, we're closed." Josef hoped he was loud enough to get the man away.

The man pulled at the door and shook the handle.

"Fuck," Josef muttered to himself. "We're closed," he said with a little more force in his voice.

The man persisted and was drawing attention from people on the street.

Josef folded up the paper and stuffed it into his pocket. He walked over to the door and unlocked it.

The man smiled as the locks were disengaged. He was tall and rail thin with a few pockmarks on his face. His eyes were blue, nearly the color of slate. A crop of thinning blonde hair adorned his head, showing a good amount of bare scalp. "Finally, someone is here," the man said. He looked around Josef and into the store. "Why have you been closed for so long?"

Josef didn't want to talk with the man. He was hoping to catch the next train home and listen to the end of the baseball game. "Sir, I'm sorry, but the store is closed." He looked up in thought. "We're going to be doing renovations, so we've closed for a few months." The lie was weak, but he didn't have time to come up with anything better.

"Yes, yes, but it's been quite some time," the man said. He continued to look over Josef and into the empty space. "I am looking for the proprietor of the store. Is he in?"

Josef looked over his shoulder into the darkness. The inane fear that something was behind him tickled the spot between his shoulder blades.

Kollmer was dead and gone. His mortal body wasn't even longer in this world, so why was Josef so scared of seeing the man behind him? It was as if he was a boy again, fearful of the monsters under the bed or in the closet. Even at a young age, he knew they weren't real, but the power of the mind was strong.

"No, I'm sorry," Josef said. He looked back at the man. "I can gladly take your name and contact information, and I will pass along your message."

Defeated, the man stopped trying to peer into the store. "No, that's fine. I'd rather not, but thank you anyway. It would've been nice to see Erik again." He looked at Josef but didn't truly *see* him. "We were close in the Old Country."

Josef's attention was piqued. The hair on his arms rose as if the room dropped in temperature. "Oh?" he croaked.

"Yes, yes," he said. The man pointed at Josef. "You have quite an accent as well." He put his finger to his lips. "Polish?"

Josef nodded and looked at the man's face, *really* looked at it. His balls tightened, pulling taut. *I know this man. That face, those eyes. The gleam in them when he thinks of Kollmer.*

The train platform.

Josef tried to block that memory from existence, but it lived on in his brain. It was a whirlwind of fear, but in the recess of his mind, the guard's face stuck. A woman and her dead, elderly mother had been in the same car with Josef and his family. The woman cradled her mother's corpse, holding her until the end of her life which was snatched away by the man in front of Josef. His pistol spat death into the grieving daughter, dispatching her like a wounded deer. Josef wondered how many others this man killed. Was his sneer the last thing terrified prisoners saw before his gun erupted?

"I figured," the man said. "I'm pretty good with accents." He looked at his watch. "Well, I must be heading out. Maybe I'll stop by again and see if Erik is here." He turned to walk away.

Could I do it again? This time, it wouldn't be the heat of the moment, but calculated murder. Murder and torment beyond anything. Well, maybe not anything. This man, and those like him, had no qualms about the torture inflicted upon the millions who'd lost their lives in the camps. Why, oh God, why, should I care about him?

"Wait," Josef said.

The man—the Nazi—stopped and turned.

Josef took a step closer, close enough to smell his aftershave. "You served with the boss?"

The Nazi's watery eyes sparkled. "Yes, for a while."

Josef knew the answer, but still had to ask. If he was going to condemn this man to death, he had to know for sure; he had to hear it spoken from his lips. Josef didn't notice at first, but he was shaking. Luckily, the Nazi didn't see it. Or if he did, he mentioned nothing.

"In…in the camp?"

"Yes, towards the end. We served together in the *Wehrmacht* for a while, but he was promoted. When he arrived in Auschwitz, he sent for me." He was looking up, reminiscing.

Josef felt ill. He put his left arm—the one with his number tattooed upon it—behind his back.

"Those were some of the best years of my life," the Nazi said. He snapped out of his daydream and looked back at Josef. His eyes narrowed as if he'd said too much. "And how exactly do you fit into the picture? Not many Poles liked the Germans, especially the Polish men."

Josef wanted to smash him in the face. It wouldn't be hard. He had at least 20 pounds on the tall Nazi, and a lifetime of built-up rage. If he didn't kill the man on the sidewalk, and died in the process, it wouldn't bother him. He should've died years ago, but the rage inside of him was alive, flickering with the flames of vengeance; a cruel side of Josef the world had never seen. Something evil brewing, but not without self-service. Josef *would* kill this man, but he would get something in return.

"I was one of the loyal ones," Josef said. He lowered his eyebrows, hoping his gaze looked conspiratorial. "My family was from the Fatherland, and they instilled national pride my entire life. I wanted to join the *Wehrmacht* in the worst way, but found out my role on the inside was much more valuable." The lies melted on his tongue like butter. "I nestled amongst the rats in the cities, telling their secrets to the soldiers. I met Kollmer in one of the ghettos where the Jews thought they could hide." He inflicted torment upon himself with his words, but he knew the pain this man would feel would make up for it.

The Nazi smiled. "Yes, good man. It was smart of you to root out the Jews. Round them up and exterminate them."

Josef thought he was going to vomit. He remembered those days in the ghettos, the untold horrors, the fear he and his family faced nightly as they heard stories from neighbors, the sound of approaching trucks.

Josef knew, at that moment, he could do what needed to be done. This was an act of survival, just as it had been that day at the gravel pits. He knew then, people had to die if he wanted to live, and he could rid the world of someone horrible, and possibly help himself.

"Listen," Josef said, moving closer. "The boss usually keeps this quiet, but I'm sure he'll be happy I invited you. He and a few friends from the Old Country had a card game downstairs." Josef pointed over his shoulder with his thumb. "It's small and very private, but I think he'll enjoy seeing you again." Josef almost checked his watch, which was on his left wrist. He caught himself, knowing if the Nazi saw his tattoo, this would all be for naught. Not only that, but it would raise suspicions about where Kollmer was, and why he'd hire a Jew to run his shop.

The Nazi lit up. A clear dribble of drool was collecting at the corner of his mouth. He used the back of his hand to wipe it away. "Oh, that would be wonderful," he said. "And what time?"

Josef did some mental calculations and blurted. "Nine, I think they start around nine. I'm usually here for the first couple of hands, but I have terrible luck with cards."

The Nazi smiled. "Oh, you should definitely play then. And the name is Karl." He reached out to shake Josef's hand.

Karl's hand looked like a serpent to Josef. It was repulsive and dangerous. He felt as if the man would pull him close and stick a Hitler youth knife right between his ribs. The man knew, he had to know he was dealing with a prisoner. Josef hoped his trembling wasn't noticeable when he reached out. Karl's hand was wet, but his grip was strong.

Finally, the contact was over.

"I'll see you tonight. Tell Kollmer I'll bring some beer too."

Josef forced a smile and fought the urge to wipe his hand on his pants. He felt sick. "Perfect, tonight at nine," Josef said.

Karl turned and left, blending in with the growing foot traffic.

Josef sat in the dark store. He was early, but certain preparations needed to be made before Karl arrived. The beer at Josef's feet was empty. He took another from the six-pack, opened the bottle with a hiss, and drank.

It was almost 8:45 p.m. Karl would be there soon, at least, he hoped. Josef, knowing this could end horribly with one mistake, wore a light, long-sleeved shirt. He had to keep his tattoo covered, just in case. If Karl were to see it at the last minute, the plan could be ruined.

The streets still had a steady flow of traffic, but Karl had yet to show. Josef looked up, gazing through the glass, watching for the Nazi. The tall man stuck out in the crowd. Even though the sun was down, Karl's watery eyes shone in the light of the streetlamps.

Josef walked over to the door and unlocked it. He pulled it open, recoiling at the sound of the bell overhead. "Karl, thank you for coming."

Karl held a full paper bag. He gave Josef a look and a sneer. "My pleasure. Forgive me for saying, but you don't look so good." He wrinkled his nose. "And, again, forgive me, you don't smell so good either."

Josef took a curious sniff at his armpits. He hadn't realized how badly he'd been sweating. When summoning Belphegor, he wasn't focused on hygiene. There was also the lingering smell of the demon on his clothes: burned shit and matches. He hoped the odor didn't drive Karl away when he reached the basement door.

"Oh, yeah. Kollmer had me doing some work around the building," Josef laughed. "I guess I'm a bit ripe, but I'm heading home after showing you the way." He stepped out of the doorway and ushered the man inside. The door twinkled as it was shut and locked.

"Eh, no worries," Karl said, adjusting the bag. "We've all been there. You wouldn't believe the smells we had to suffer through at the camps." Again, he wrinkled his nose. "Filthy people."

Josef had to fight himself. It took every ounce of willpower not to strike Karl. As good as that would've felt, he knew the man's fate was much worse than a broken nose.

"So, how did you two make it over without getting caught?" Josef asked.

Karl ran his finger over a grimy display case, sneering at the filth. "Oh, you know. Luck and a lot of money. There were plenty of people after us—any of us—to put on display during their little trials. It was nothing more than a witch hunt, chasing down soldiers and killing them. A few of us were fortunate, establishing connections with sympathizers in South America. We escaped the war zone with ease. If you lingered, you risked the chance of being captured by the Allies, or even worse, the Soviets. People say the Nazis were the worst ones." He laughed and waved his hand. "They've never seen a prisoner of the Red Army."

Josef opened the door leading downstairs. "I'm sure they were just as bad, if not worse," he said. "My people, the Poles, have long fought the Soviets. We know their hatred and ferocity." He snapped on a light as they made their way down.

The smell increased, but Karl said nothing. Ahead was the locked door, the door where Hell lived.

Josef fished the keyring out of his pocket. His hands were shaking, but Karl was looking around the dim room.

"Why in the fuck would he have this game down here? This is quite dreary if I say so."

Josef forced a laugh. "Yeah, he's well aware, but some players—like yourself—are defectors. Even though it's been almost a decade since the end of the war, many are still afraid of being found out." He selected the key and slid it into the lock. "I've

FOR THE BETTER

even heard rumors of the Jews sending out squads to kill or capture former Nazis." Josef opened the door.

"Pff, a Jew hit squad? Please, they are weak people with no spine for murder," Karl said. He peered into the gloom, noticing only the candles lit. "What in the fuck are you doing, Kollmer? Is this any way to greet an old friend?"

Josef moved behind the man, guiding him forward. He almost froze, stopping with fear.

The demon was in the center of the circle of candles, but he was smart. Belphegor hung just beyond the edge of the light. A faint outline of his hell-born body could be seen. His flesh glistened in the orange glow.

Intrigued by the candles, Karl moved closer.

Josef turned on the lights, hoping the man was close enough to be shoved into the circle.

Karl froze. There was nothing else he could do.

Belphegor rushed forward, bouncing off the protective circle. His body glistened and writhed as masses of bugs slithered from the pustules weeping on his flesh.

"H…how?" Karl muttered, his face locked in fear.

Josef couldn't help but stare alongside the man. The demon's gaze was that of a cobra—inviting and intoxicating. Looking at him was the same as looking at a horrid car crash with corpses strewn about. Josef knew he shouldn't stare, but it was too hard not to.

"Come closer, meat," Belphegor growled. His three-clawed hand was pressed against the circle. "Come to me and suffer your fate."

The gravelly sound of the demon's voice snapped both men out of their trances.

Karl turned as Josef loaded up his kick.

Josef glimpsed fear on Karl's face. It was pure and one Josef had seen countless times. It was the mask of fear he'd seen on thousands of bodies as they were thrown into trucks or loaded into the hungry mouth of the crematorium. He knew he shouldn't have been happy about what he was about to do, but he was. He kicked.

The kick caught Karl in the hip, just about folding the thin man in half. He shot backward with his back leading into the circle.

Belphegor drooled and waited for the glorious second when the man would break the plane.

Karl entered the lair of the demon.

Belphegor's claws pierced Karl's lower back, sinking deep into his flesh. Karl's hands remained outside of the boundary for just a moment, grasping at Josef, who might as have been on the surface of the moon.

"There's no escape, meat," Belphegor growled. Bugs poured from his mouth. They grated over his wet, drooling tongue, slapping to the ground.

"Please, no!" Karl screamed. Blood ran down his flanks as the demon pulled harder.

FOR THE BETTER

Belphegor, with his free hand, grabbed Karl's shoulder. Bone crunched and flesh parted as the demon yanked and ripped Karl's arm off. A shower of gore sprayed against the protective barrier; Karl was fully inside the protection. Clothing and flesh tore, leaving a ragged, wet chasm where the man's arm used to reside.

With a firm grasp on Karl's flank, Belphegor crammed the severed arm into his mouth. Bones crunched and blood ran, but the demon ate with glee.

Josef could only watch in horror. When he'd killed Kollmer, it seemed to happen so quickly. It was brutal, but over in seconds.

The demon was taking his time with Karl, savoring the kill and relishing in the pallor of Josef's face. This would not be over quickly. Belphegor grabbed Karl around the neck, but gently enough to not spill blood. Not that it would have mattered at that point; the ragged hole where his arm used to be was pumping burgundy. The demon kicked Karl low in the back, just under his spine. With a pop, the man's pelvis shattered, distorting his hips.

Karl was pale, but still screamed at the brutal pain washing over his damaged body. He folded backward and dropped to his knees, as his pelvis could no longer hold his weight.

With the tall man much lower, Belphegor put his face close to Karl's, but his eyes never left Josef. "Mmm, this is good meat," the demon said.

A thick, black worm crawled from his mouth, finding its way to Karl's nose. Its body, lubricated by slime, entered the Nazi's nostril.

Josef looked away as the offending creature bulged and wriggled, burrowing deeper into Karl's sinus cavity.

Belphegor licked Karl's blood-splattered face, tasting his flesh. "Perfect." The demon's mouth opened and opened, growing wider. With every creak of his jaw, Belphegor's mouth seemed to sprout more and more teeth, each one more jagged than the last.

Karl's life was fading, but in the last glimmer before death took him, there was fear in his eyes.

The demon closed its jaws over Karl's entire head and bit.

Karl's body was released, and fell wet and heavy to the floor. Blood pumped from the stump where his head was only moments earlier.

Belphegor chewed, crunching the skull in his mouth like a hard candy. Bits of scalp, brain, bone, and gore were revealed with every crushing bite. The demon swallowed and crouched down, setting upon the rest of the corpse, the 'meat' of Karl.

Whether in fear or morbidity, Josef's gaze was locked. He watched the demon intentionally pull Karl's genitals off, laughing as he ate them. He watched the demon plunge his fingers into the cooling chest cavity, ripping it open and feasting on the wet innards. He watched Belphegor bathe himself in bile and stomach matter, squeezing a bouquet of viscera over his mouth like a ripe orange.

Josef's gaze slowly relaxed, like waking from a nightmare. He saw the waiting holy water and moved to grab it.

Belphegor watched him, but didn't slow his feast. "Ah, I have to leave so soon?" the demon asked with a loop of shit-smeared intestine hanging from his mouth. "More meat, Pet Jew. More. Fucking. Meat!" Belphegor rushed the barrier again, and again, the protection held strong. He sneered and paced like a lion.

Josef threw the holy water on the demon and listened to it sizzle.

Belphegor smiled as he shifted, morphing back into slime and slithering into the stone.

Josef felt weak. Spots danced in his vision. He thought he might pass out. He lowered himself to the floor and put his head in his hands. Slowly, he pulled out a pack of cigarettes and lit one. The smoke rose, and the nicotine flooded his system. He stared at the rising smoke. With every puff, he saw something in the floating milkiness.

The face of the demon.

Schatzi whined.

Josef slowly awoke. A ray of sunlight warmed his face as he slowly came back to reality. His dreams were violent and disturbing, but luckily, he didn't remember them. The aftereffect left a feeling like oil on his brain, but the memories fleeted away into the ether.

Schatzi barked and spun, wagging her tail hard enough to hit the nightstand.

Josef stretched and prepared himself for the myriad of aches and pains associated with his growing age. He stretched…and felt nothing. He felt amazing. Nothing creaked or popped, not even a wince of pain.

The memory of the night before came rushing back to him.

The demon and the Nazi.

It was all crystal clear in his mind's eye: Karl, another orchestrator of death and torment, was given what he deserved. Belphegor, relishing in the destruction of the man, tore him to shreds, taking his earthly body to another realm.

A sacrifice for the good of Josef.

Josef looked at his hands. They looked the same, yet *different.* Something about the elasticity of the skin and the lack of bulging veins; even the color seemed healthier. He threw back the sheet and ran into the bathroom.

Schatzi followed, whimpering to be let out.

The aging man looked in the mirror. The difference was subtle, but it was there. Josef's face didn't look nearly as worn or tired. Even the little paunch he'd got from too many hotdogs seemed flatter. The change in his appearance wasn't drastic, and most people wouldn't even notice, but he did.

Maybe a few coworkers, his officemate for sure, but the changes were just subtle enough to go undetected.

Schatzi scratched at his leg.

"Okay, girl, let's go," he said, looking down at her.

He glanced back at his reflection in abject horror. For just a flash—a split second—his face was gone. In the mirror was the unholy visage of the demon, Belphegor. His bathroom had been replaced and, in its stead, a disturbing level of Hell. Geysers of fire erupted, tormented souls were harassed by hellish imps, vile sex and death, in every imaginable way, unfolded in front of him. And then, it was gone. It was as if the vision never occurred, like a bad dream floating away.

His youthful heart thumped wildly in his chest as he looked back at his image. Slowly, he left the bathroom, Schatzi none the wiser.

Josef took his dog out into the warmth of the early afternoon, breathing in a lungful of fresh air. Even breathing felt better. For every painless step he took, Josef knew what the cost was. He'd taken a human life—another human life. It was something most people never experienced, but he had. And when his body didn't ache walking down the street, Josef didn't care, not in the least.

DANIEL J. VOLPE

29th, August 1971

It has been nearly 20 years since I opened this book. Truth be told, it's been a good period in my life. Schatzi, my sweet girl, lived longer than any dog had business living. I'm not sure exactly how old she was when I found her dead in bed, but she lived with me for 17 years. Since the day with the demon, she hadn't had so much as a sniffle and died—as far as I could tell—peacefully in her sleep. Oh, how I envied her. To just close your eyes and not awaken. Slipping into a quiet death, warm in bed, with dreams running wild. Not me, no. Still, I'm here and shockingly, better than ever. The day after I killed my second Nazi, the world looked different. The colors were brighter and smells more potent. My eyes were that of a man a quarter of my age, and I have yet to need glasses. It was like I was reborn through death. A death that still lingers in the back of my brain, but one I feel no remorse over. Karl was an evil man, ranking alongside Kollmer and the other men and women of the death camps. Still, I took a life in exchange for my own.

Since that day, I have not seen the demon. Even in my dreams, he's rarely there. And when he is, I defeat him handily, shunning him. It's safe to say that I've not summoned him in almost 2 decades and, until recently, haven't even had the urge. The stone prison in which he lives sits in my basement, dark and discarded. When I moved from my apartment in

FOR THE BETTER

Yonkers to the house I'm currently writing from, I knew I couldn't leave the stone behind. Kollmer's store was the perfect front to hide the talisman, but once my promotion was finalized, I knew I had to leave. I can still feel the abhorrent touch of the black rock. I handled it like a live bomb, carefully and under the cover of darkness, moving it from the basement of the store. Now, it sits alone in the dark, surrounded by boxes of memories.

Why now, after all of these years, am I writing in this journal again? The urge. The urge to summon him again; to allow the demon to feed. And this time it is not to save myself, but others. I hope.

There is a new darkness spreading around the world. A new evil that's churning up men and women and spitting them out. The US has sent many sons to fight and die in a foreign land, but a lot of them come home. And some of them don't come home the same.

The suburbs are a wondrous place, often reminding me of the old country. My neighborhood is as American as can be, but there is a black underbelly, no matter where we go. My neighbors are great, but one man, I fear, is evil. He was one of those boys who went overseas and came back different, or so I'm told. I never knew Peter Ward before the war, but I know him now. I know evil when I see it. Every person has a mean streak in them, and the darkness occasionally slips out. But the good people don't lose control. Rather, we control the anger, finding new outlets for it and never letting it consume us. For some men, Peter being one of them, the evil is what they know. It's the warm darkness that cradles them, lovingly, nurturing their desire to hurt.

And for that reason, I'm writing. Writing to look inside myself for what I should do. I've fought monsters before and won, but again, I'm faced with another challenge. Do I side with the evil to best evil, or let the world unfold as it was meant to be? Or is the Hell-beast in my basement part of the grand scheme? Was it left to me for a reason of greater good? For that, I'm sure.

Please, God, if you're there, grant me strength.

Please.

CHAPTER 6

The late summer day was a slice of heaven. Fat clouds hung heavy in the blue sky, offering a wandering shade. The sharp tang of fresh-cut grass was rich in the air. In the distance, a dog barked, but Josef couldn't see it.

He sat outside with a cool drink next to him and a book in his hand. It was Saturday, the last one of the summer. Over the years, he'd been spoiled by his teacher's schedule. He couldn't imagine life any other way. Working during the summer seemed almost barbaric, especially as he entered his 70s. Even though he was 71 years old, not a single person in their right mind would make him out for that. Many people mistook him for a man decades younger, and rightfully so. The death of Karl not only cured his ailments, but was seemingly a fountain of youth. Josef had no disillusions of living forever, the death of Schatzi solidified that, but he didn't think it would be much of a problem to live old and die peacefully. As badly as he wanted to see Ola and the boys again, the will to live overruled everything.

Josef put his thumb in his book and reached down to grab his drink. The unsweetened tea was bitter and the lemon slice floating on the melting ice added just a hint of tang. He sipped and put the glass back down. Drops of condensation made a dark ring on the deck where the glass rested. He wiped his hand on his pants before reopening his book.

The sound of bells made him look up. A wide smile split his face, even though he couldn't see the source of the sound. Josef pulled his bookmark from his shirt pocket and slipped it between the pages as he looked towards the ringing.

Cindy Ward came around the corner of the block. The streamers on her handlebars blew behind her and her little thumb worked the battered bell. She sang a pop song, one Josef didn't know, as her short red hair danced in her face. Cindy shook her head, getting the loose strands of hair out of her eyes.

She saw Josef sitting outside and beamed. With one hand still controlling the bike, she waved with the other. "Hiya, Mr. Lazer!" she yelled.

Josef stood and stretched his back. He set his book down on the chair and picked up his drink. He waved back, but didn't yell. Only children could scream across the street, not old men.

He'd lived in the house for only a few days before he met the young girl and her parents. Schatzi was still alive and spry as ever, even if she was only days away from death. Even though he had a yard, Josef and Schatzi still enjoyed taking walks. It was good for both of them and kept them young.

Being new to the area, Josef hadn't quite found his bearings. The entire move, plus his promotion, had all been a whirlwind. Not to mention the fact he was transporting a chunk of stone containing one of the seven princes of Hell.

FOR THE BETTER

Josef and Schatzi had been walking around the block when a little voice, squeaking with joy, yelled from an open garage.

Schatzi, who'd been sniffing for a spot to poop, looked up at the little red-headed girl rushing from the garage door. The little dog, her bowel movement forgotten, began wagging her tail as the girl approached.

"Cindy, ask the man first," a woman, presumably the girl's mother, said.

"Hiya, mister. I'm Cindy. Can I pet your doggy?" the girl asked, as she crouched down to Schatzi's level.

Schatzi had a burst of energy, licking Cindy's hands as the girl petted the petite dog.

Josef smiled and laughed. "Sure thing, Cindy. This is Schatzi."

Cindy looked up at him. "Schatzi? That's a weird name."

If you only knew the whole story of this doggy, little Cindy, Josef thought.

"I'm so sorry," the mother said, crossing the street to join her daughter. "She loves dogs."

Both adults watched as Cindy and Schatzi became friends.

"Oh, I'm Janet," she said, extending her hand.

Josef took her hand in his.

She had a thin build and chestnut hair pulled back into a ponytail. Her cheeks were dark with dirt and her brow was damp with sweat.

"Josef," he said, shaking her hand.

Schatzi and Cindy played, laughing and yipping, until something caused the girl to stop. Her freckled face went pale and her head, along with her mother's, snapped at the sound of a loud exhaust.

"Come on, Cindy," Janet said, grabbing her daughter by the arm.

Cindy sprung up, still reaching down to stroke Schatzi's head. "Bye, Schatzi," she said before looking at Josef. "Oh, and bye, Mr…"

"Lazerowitz, but you can call me Mr. Lazer, if you'd like."

Cindy smiled, but the growl of the vehicle grew ever louder.

Janet pulled her daughter back towards the house, whispering to her along the way. The mother and daughter entered the open garage just as a battered pickup truck rounded the corner.

The old Chevy sounded mean and looked even worse. Its body was dented and scratched, and the driver didn't look much better. A man with a shock of red hair sat behind the wheel as the truck screeched to a halt in the driveway. He stepped out with a beer in his hand, upended the rest of it into his mouth, and tossed the empty can into the bed of the truck.

Josef watched him, close enough to see the intoxication in his eyes.

The man looked at Josef and his dog, his gaze narrowing. "Can I help you?" he slurred. Red stubble adorned his face. He was thin, but covered in corded muscle. A small paunch pressed against his stomach, the beginning of a full-on beer belly.

"Oh, ah, I'm the new neighbor. I was just walking my dog around, trying to explore the area."

The man didn't soften, but rather looked at his wife and daughter in the garage. "Making friends when you should've been cleaning?"

Janet forced a smile.

In that instant, Josef realized the smudge on her face wasn't dirt, but a bruise.

"Oh no, we were just taking a little break when he came by." Janet pointed at Josef. "Peter, this is Josef, our new neighbor."

Peter's eyes snapped back to Josef. They started on his face, then lowered to his left arm—the arm with the numbers tattooed on it.

Peter sucked his teeth. "Welcome to the neighborhood." He turned back to his wife and daughter, who were bustling something around in the garage. "Finish this up. I'll be inside. It's been a shit day and I'm gonna need you to help me work out some of this frustration later." Peter grabbed Janet and pulled her in. He squeezed her behind and forced his tongue down her throat.

She gently pushed him away, plastering another fake smile upon her face. "Sure thing, Pete. Why don't you go inside and let us finish up out here."

Pete grunted, slapped her in the ass, and walked into the house.

That had been over a year ago.

Cindy had grown in the year since he'd moved in. He supposed all little kids do, but he hadn't been around one for over a year since he'd lost his sons. She was still the little girl that he'd met when he first moved in, and probably always would be, at least to him.

She put both hands back on the handlebars and bore down on the peddles. Her bare legs pumped hard and her auburn hair flew behind her, mimicking the streamers.

A year earlier, Schatzi would've been wagging and excited to see her friend, but the old girl had passed. Josef found her dead in her bed, surrounded by her toys, only a few days after moving into the house. He didn't know the depth of a dog's psyche, but she looked happy and at peace.

Cindy slid to a halt in Josef's driveway, and gently laid her bike down. Her brow was sweaty, and even though it was early in the day, the temperature was steadily creeping up.

The summer was always a haven for most teachers, but it could be a double-edged sword for Josef. Yes, he enjoyed his time off, and not having to commute or sit through meetings, but it all came at a price.

Everything did.

He was alone with his thoughts and demons. The demons in his mind, and the even more terrifying one in the basement. He found himself drinking some nights, sitting outside listening to the bugs and sounds of the neighborhood. Most evenings were peaceful, but an errant scream or backfire in the dark would set his old heart racing. The night he and his family were ripped from their home in Poland would play over and over across his intoxicated mind, pulling him back to the stinking train car. He knew, as an administrator, that his summer vacation wasn't as long as that of a teacher any longer, but it was long enough for his mind to play tricks on him.

Josef smiled at Cindy and stood. He wiped off the chair next to him, even though there was nothing visible on it.

Cindy took a seat in the shade. "Boy, it's a hot one today," she said, and looked at his glass, cool condensation running down the sides.

Josef, realizing what the girl was getting at, stood. "Oh, I'm sorry. Let me get you a drink."

Cindy gave him a gapped grin. "That would be great, Mr. Lazer. Thank you."

Josef disappeared inside the house and returned moments later with a glass of iced tea filled to the top with floating ice cubes.

"Thank you," Cindy said, sipping carefully. Her sips turned into gulps as she tilted her head back to allow the cold drink to slide down her throat.

That was when Josef saw the bruises around her neck. They were subtle, like they might have been healing, but his wandering eyes, which remained sharp over the years, found others. Fresh ones on her upper arm just peeked out from her short sleeves.

Ice tinkled in the glass as the girl finished.

She let out a resounding, "Ahh," and set it down on the table. Her eyes found his and her smile faltered. "What?" she asked. Cindy looked at her shoulder, as if she might have a bee on her or something. "Is there something on me?" she looked around. "Do I have something on my face?"

Josef fought out a smile, trying to ease the girl's insecurities. "No, no, nothing on your face or buzzing around you. It's just…" He let it hang in the air, focusing his eyes on her neck and back on her arms. Sitting as she was, the offending marks were all but covered, but he'd seen them, and he'd seen more than enough violence to know what they were.

Their neighborhood, like every other in the country, had its share of problems. Crime wasn't one of them, but people had their demons. The Wards liked to air out their secrets, well, at least Peter did. Drunk, loud, and mean were his only three speeds, and he seemed to be fully revved up most of the time.

In the year Josef lived in the house, he learned a bit about Mr. Ward. Most of it was from Barry, another widower, albeit much younger than Josef. Barry had been injured in a machine shop accident, leaving him with a rather painful looking limp, but he did his best to get around the neighborhood. His big ears and open mouth made him the town gossip. One of the few times Josef and Barry's walking schedule lined up, the two men talked the entire time. Well, mostly Barry, but Josef listened. He went on about the neighbors, airing their dirty laundry one house at a time.

FOR THE BETTER

Josef didn't much care about who was cheating on whom, or who had a gambling debt. What he did care about was the Wards, mainly Cindy and Janet. He already knew enough about Peter, but was always intrigued to know what made men evil. Nazi or not, some people were just plain bad.

"The war did it to him," Barry said.

Peter wasn't nearly old enough for World War 2, but there had been another, no-so-grand, fight in the Pacific, a fight that was hotly contested on the nightly news in the country of Vietnam.

"Now, I didn't know him before he went over, but I know him now, and let's just say the war did something to him. Unless he was a sunofabitch before then, maybe I'm wrong."

Barry continued to blather on for the rest of the walk, but Josef paid little attention. He'd seen many men like Peter when he was in Auschwitz, men who needed little excuse to hurt others, men who enjoyed the pain on the faces of their victims. Josef was eternally grateful to the soldiers who had fought the evil in the world, but he knew all men weren't created equal. Some men relished the power of war. The only problem was that Janet and Cindy weren't the enemy; they were Peter's family.

Josef sighed, knowing he and Cindy were friends. But he also knew children. Even so, he had to ask her. "Cindy," he said. His old eyes were kind and soft, with just a touch of wateriness to them. "What happened to your neck and arm?"

The girl's smile wavered, but didn't fall. She was used to lying and being caught off guard. But the one thing she couldn't control was her eyes. They were truly the windows to the soul, and hers was hurting. Fear and pain snapped across her young face, even though she smiled. Absently, she reached up and touched her neck, killing time while she came up with an excuse.

"Oh, this?" she asked, rubbing at her neck. A bruised arm was much easier to lie about, as opposed to strangulation marks on the lithe neck of a little girl. "I…I, um…" She looked away from Josef, her mind racing. And then she snapped back to him with the lie on her lips. "I was at June Martin's house—you wouldn't know her; she was in my class last year—and we were playing rodeo. I was the horse, and she was the cowgirl. While I was on my bike, she threw a rope around my neck." Cindy forced a laugh and rubbed the back of her head. "I guess that wasn't the best idea now, was it? She yanked me clean off my bike, and knocked the darn—excuse the language, Mr. Lazer—wind right out of me. I must've gotten the bruises on my arms at the same time." Cindy quickly picked up her drink and slurped the melted ice. Her hands shook, and she watched the liquid rush into her mouth. A little dribbled down her chin as the ice cubes slid around.

Slowly, Josef picked up his glass and drank. His was watery, but cool. He sipped the thin layer of ice water that had formed at the top, getting down to the tea. Such was life, full of layers. Some of them were good through and through, while others were not. Josef hoped this layer in the life of young Cindy was the worst she'd experience, that maybe her father would be a father and realize the gift he'd been given to have his wife and child to love and nurture, and to love him. Josef hoped and prayed at that moment, under the August sun, that life would work out just fine for Cindy.

Deep down, he knew his prayers would go unanswered.

Chapter 7

Heavy thunderheads roiled in the sky, but didn't burst. The dark clouds, ominous and foreboding, swirled and blackened, turning the summer day into night. Josef looked out the window, up at the sky. His porch was empty, and he'd pulled the chairs and small table into the house. They sat out of place in the living room, but at least they were safe. Every so often, when a peal of lightning would flash and thunder roll, he'd look around for Schatzi. It took him a few times before he'd remembered she was gone from this world and, hopefully, in a better place.

Something else—actually *someone* else—had been missing for quite a while. It had been over a week since Josef had last seen Cindy. He knew school was on the horizon and little girls were all a buzz with buying new clothes and finding out what class they were in the next year. While he didn't expect her to spend every waking moment on his porch sipping drinks and chewing the fat, he hadn't seen her at all, not even racing by his house, streamers blowing in the breeze. Not a glimpse of her when Janet, or even Peter, came home. It was as if the girl had disappeared. Josef thought little of it at first, but as the days passed and still no Cindy, he worried.

Every day, Peter's big truck would come racing down the street, swerving, and screeching to a halt in the driveway. Josef would look across the street and, even in the dusk, he could tell Peter swayed with intoxication.

Josef took his eyes from the swirling storm clouds and looked at the Ward house. It sat quiet and unoccupied. Neither vehicle was there, and not a single light was on. He hadn't seen Janet's car since the previous morning, nor Peter's obnoxious truck.

As if he'd summoned her, Janet's car turned the corner and headed towards their driveway.

Josef's heart raced. Another shattering blast of thunder echoed in the heavens, and to the old man—the survivor—it was like a gunshot or a starter pistol.

Before he even realized what he was doing, Josef opened his front door.

Janet pulled into the driveway, but didn't exit the car.

Josef stood on his porch watching, praying the back door of the car would open and Cindy would bound out. He knew she'd stand and stare, watching the storm, fascinated by it. She'd wait for the rain to fall and dance in the puddles with the carefree nature of youth. All the while, Janet would stand under their awning, shouting to the girl to get in the house. She'd smile at her daughter's love of life, even though her words would be terse. They'd hug—a tight one, to get her mother wet—and laugh as they went into the house.

The back door of the car didn't open, and Cindy didn't get out. Janet did, and even in the storm's gloom, Josef saw the damage on her face. At first glance, his mind tried to convince him what he saw wasn't real. His brain kept telling him it was the play of the shadows thanks to the storm clouds, but he wasn't stupid. No, his brain was conditioned for violence and had witnessed some of the most horrific things known to man; what he saw was real.

Before Josef could stop himself, he marched across the street. He felt light, as if he were floating, almost an ethereal feeling as his shoes made marks on the soft grass.

Janet didn't see him, or if she did, she didn't notice him. She tossed her purse strap over one shoulder and slid a pair of large sunglasses over her face. They weren't enough to cover the swelling on her cheeks.

"Janet!" Josef yelled.

Thunder boomed in the sky and the treetops danced.

She didn't hear him and pushed her car door closed. Janet, with her keys still in hand, turned her back to Josef and started towards the front door.

Josef was never much of an athlete. Although he didn't feel his age, his body still wasn't a fan of running. He picked up his pace, not looking as he crossed the street. "Janet!" he yelled again, and this time, the woman paused.

Janet looked over her shoulder at her neighbor, who was in an oddly paced jog. Her shoulders hunched as if she were about to be struck, and her feet shifted.

Josef closed the distance, hoping he wouldn't spook her into running away from him. He'd seen fear; he'd felt fear, the fear of a gun pointed at the back of your head, the itch knowing any of the sadists wearing a Death's Head emblem could kill you for any reason. To live year-round in constant fear was something he'd escaped. If only his neighbor could escape the same fate.

Janet didn't run, but looked up the street. The roll of thunder was loud, almost as obnoxious as Peter's truck, but not nearly as ominous.

Slightly winded from his short jog, he took a few calming breaths, but his heart wouldn't slow.

Janet's face, even with the sunglasses, was worse up close. Her nose was bruised and had a butterfly bandage over it. The break must not have been that severe as it didn't look deformed, but Josef suspected it was broken. Both cheeks were swollen and dark with bruising, and even through the tint of the glasses, Josef could see her eyes were blackened.

The look on Josef's face, the two tiny mirrors of her lenses reflecting his horrified look, broke Janet. Tears ran from behind her glasses as she let out a wail.

He stepped forward and allowed the woman to collapse in his arms. Her sobs were deep and mournful—sobs that Josef had cried himself only a few decades earlier: the pained cries of loss.

His heart rattled like a machine gun, and he wanted to pull her away and ask about Cindy. Where was the sweet, freckled little girl who'd he'd come to love over the past year? What did the monster pretending to be her father do to her, to *them*?

Janet's sobs didn't slow, but she picked her head up to look Josef in the face.

"Come on, let's go inside before the neighbors start talking," he said. Josef didn't know if it was supposed to be a joke, or if he was serious, but it felt right.

Janet sniffled and winced at the pain, but nodded.

Together, they walked into the house.

She took her glasses off, revealing what Josef had suspected. Her face looked like she'd gone twelve rounds with a boxer. Both eyes were busted up, but the left one had suffered the brunt. A jagged row of stitches held her brow closed.

Rage. Pure, white-hot rage poured over Josef like lava. He felt it running through his body as if his blood were boiling. There would be no more lies, no more games to play. He needed to know. "What the fuck did he do to you? Where's Cindy?"

Janet's tears slowed, but at the mention of her daughter, fresh ones rose anew. "He...he—" she started, but had to stop. Snot, pink with blood, ran down her face. Not caring about formalities, she wiped her nose with the back of her hand. "She was putting her bike away and...and scratched his truck."

Josef was taken aback. Peter's truck was a busted-up piece of shit to begin with; another scratch would hardly be noticeable. He wanted to pry and ask more, to usher the answers from her, but he knew he had to let her take her time.

"The son of a bitch lost it. He took a swing at her, but she was fast, too fast for his drunk ass. That only pissed him off even more. Cindy ran into the house. The fear in her eyes is something I'll never forget. I tried to stop him, but his first punch broke my nose, dropping me to the floor. She ran and was cornered, stopping at the top of the basement steps." She was no longer looking at him, but staring off, remembering the atrocity committed on her baby. "The door was open, and he didn't even fucking hesitate. He fucking kicked her, Josef. He kicked our baby, no, *my* baby, down the stairs." She stopped talking, hard swallowed, and began again, "Then he came back to me." Janet touched her face, wincing as if wanting to be in pain. "But Cindy…" the sobs made her shoulders rise and fall and more bloody snot ran. This time, she let it run past her mouth and down her chin. "She's been in a coma since. Her brain is bleeding, and we don't know if she'll ever wake up." Janet's knees buckled and she fell.

Josef did his best to cradle her fall, but hit the ground with her. He didn't speak. He didn't have to. Instead, he held her tight, letting her get it all out, to unleash her sorrow on him.

Outside, the storm broke open. Torrents of rain and gouts of lightning ripped across the sky. Inside the house, another storm was brewing. This one, inside the chest of an old man.

An old man with a dark secret.

FOR THE BETTER

Josef sat in his living room with a glass of bourbon. A lone lamp was the only light source, barely enough to chase away the shadows of night. The storm had blown through hours earlier, causing the power to flicker, but the grid held strong. Branches were strewn about his yard, but the large pines that bordered his property held fast.

Josef's shirt was still wet, not from the rain, but from the tears and snot of his injured neighbor. His tears were kept at bay, held deep in reserve. Josef didn't shed them. He let them sit and fester. He turned his grief into hatred, something he didn't think he'd ever have to do again.

He wasn't naïve that evil existed everywhere, but when he'd been liberated from the camp, he'd hoped he'd seen the last of true evil. But no, here he was in suburban America, watching the destruction of two—no, three—lives. Josef didn't know if the third life was his own, or that of Peter, and truly, he didn't care. Josef had done things—in and out of the camp—that he knew damned his soul to the pits of Hell. And he, more than anyone else, knew what awaited in the lake of fire.

Below, in the darkness of the basement, Josef heard a scratching. It was faint, almost something that lived in his brain. He strained his ears, listening to the house groan and shift. There was a scratching...and laughing. The smell of burning shit and matches permeated the floorboards, rising to his old nose.

Josef sniffled, not realizing he had a trickle of snot running free.

And then, the smell was gone. The house was still, with not a creak or rumble, but Josef knew. He knew what he'd summoned and what he was going to do. At least, what he was going to *try* to do.

Thunder rolled and Josef perked up. It wasn't thunder he heard; it was the rumble of a truck. A truck which carried a human monster.

Headlights lit the dark street as Peter's truck turned. He must've hit the gas a little too hard because the tires squealed on the wet pavement. If the neighborhood hadn't known he was home from the sound of the exhaust, the burnout was sure to alert them.

Josef grabbed what was left of his drink and threw it back. The liquor burned, and he had to force the image of hellfire from his mind. He slammed the glass down on the end table and stood. He adjusted his belt, which was a little heavier thanks to an artifact he'd stolen from Kollmer. After a few deep breaths, he steadied his jangled nerves and went to the front door.

The streetlights cast buttery puddles of light up and down the block. Peter's big truck was partially parked on his driveway and lawn; it was still running when Josef stepped outside.

Josef could see him in the truck, his form was lit up by the glow of the dash. A demon in his own right, illuminated in the cab.

Abruptly, the engine stopped. The echo of the rumbling exhaust died on the houses and the door swung open. Two beer bottles fell, shattering on the driveway, as Peter stumbled out of the truck.

Josef was nearly across the street, but didn't want to sneak up on the volatile man. When he was close enough to speak without yelling, he would announce himself. He didn't want to make a scene, nor did he want anyone seeing Peter with him. Josef knew that was almost an impossibility, but he didn't think the neighborhood would miss the man.

"Peter," Josef said. He was far enough away to not get punched by the drunk man, but close enough to not yell.

Peter spun, showing incredible balance for someone who appeared to be hammered drunk. A slight stumble, which was aided by his truck, was the only inebriation he showed. "Huh?" the drunk man said, peering into the gloom.

Josef hadn't yet stepped into the circle of light cast by the streetlamp. "It's me, Josef."

Peter sneered like he'd smelled something offensive. "Oh. Can I help you?" he asked with venom in each word.

Josef stepped into the light. He didn't know why, but he made a point to show his empty hands; it was ingrained in him when dealing with predators to show them you're no threat. "Yes, I was hoping you could. This damned storm knocked a huge branch onto my back patio. I was hoping you could help me cut it and move it real fast."

Peter was taken aback. It was dark and a slight mist hung in the air. He looked almost offended that Josef would ask for his help, let alone at such an hour.

Peter opened his mouth to reply, and Josef played his ace in the hole. "I just grabbed a fresh case of beer. I know sometimes men can work up a thirst with hard work. Drink what you want and take the rest when we're done. For a strong guy like yourself, it should only take a few minutes. I just have to get the old chainsaw revved up, and that's it."

The mention of free beer changed something in Peter's face. Josef knew if there was actually beer involved, Peter would just drink and leave, not bothering to help.

Peter smiled. "Well, I suppose it would be the neighborly thing to do." He slammed the door of his truck and began walking towards Josef.

Josef's breath was stuck in his throat like cotton. His tongue was dry, and his world slowed down. It felt like he was seeing another demon walking towards him in the growing dark.

Peter shuffled closer. His gait was that of a man who had already had a few drinks, but Josef knew Peter's night was just beginning. The streetlights didn't give off much, but more than enough illumination shone down to let Josef see the cuts and marks on Peter's knuckles.

FOR THE BETTER

White rage flooded Josef. In his mind's eye, he could see this man—this full-grown man—beating the shit out of his wife. Were the boots Peter wore the same ones he was wearing when he kicked Cindy down the stairs? Josef was vibrating with hatred, but his heart was thumping smoothly. He had a job to do.

"Any word on Cindy?" Josef asked. He hadn't intended to mention the girl, but it just came out. He knew it was a mistake the moment it left his lips.

Peter paused, just for a second, but the shift on his face was there, as if something evil was lurking beneath the skin. He shook his head.

"I guess my big-mouth wife has been talking again, huh?" Peter flexed his hands, curling them into fists.

Josef didn't know if it was a trick of his mind, or if it made a sound, but he could've sworn he heard the tendons creak in the man's fists.

"Oh, no. I hadn't seen Cindy for a while and approached her, cornered her even."

They joined up in the street and were walking towards Josef's house. One of them would never leave there again. Josef hoped it wasn't him.

"Yeah," Peter drawled. "I've noticed you taking a liking to my girls."

Both men entered the house, Josef in the lead.

"Well, they're both wonderful, Peter," Josef said, welcoming him across the threshold.

Peter looked around at the clean, sparse house with a sneer on his face. "Yeah, just fucking wonderful." Without another word, he walked to the kitchen and pulled open the fridge. The thought of free beer was enough to drive him on.

Josef stood by the basement steps. His rage was building, but he was steady. He had to stick to the plan. "You know, I lost my entire family in the war." He didn't say the camps, even though he had the dreaded number tattooed on his left forearm. "I loved them dearly, and didn't realize how much until they were gone."

His eyes burned as he thought back to life before the camp, the days of fun with his boys, Piotr and Michal, playing at the park while Ola sat watching, her book lying open in her lap, untouched as she watched her family enjoy a perfect fall day. And then, her eyes would lock on Josef's and something would be exchanged in the brief interaction, a knowing that they were living in perfection. And that night, after the boys were tired out and asleep, Josef and Ola would make love like they were young, with a passion and intensity reserved for youthful lovers. Josef would've given anything to spend eternity in that day.

Peter was only half listening, if that, as he rummaged through Josef's sparse refrigerator. "Tough break," he said, knocking down a jar of something. The dim bulb illuminated his face as he turned back to Josef. "Well, I still have my family. And once Cindy gets over this bump on the head, we might pack up and set off west." Peter slammed the door shut. Jars and bottles fell, causing Josef to cringe. "Say, where the fuck is the beer? I'm not working for free and I'm already thirsty."

Josef took a deep breath, steadying his nerves. "I'm sorry," he said. "I have another fridge in the basement. It's a full case, so I didn't want to stuff it up here." He rubbed the back of his neck, feigning guilt. In reality, Josef was just trying to keep his composure. He knew what awaited them in the basement, and it sure as hell wasn't a case of beer.

Peter stomped towards him, a look of disgust on his face. "Here?" he asked, pointing to the basement door.

"Yeah, just down the steps. Can't miss it." Josef opened the door, wafting a gust of putrid air.

Peter stepped into the threshold and stopped. "*Bleh*, it smells like shit down there. Did your waste line back up or something?" Even the stink of a demon couldn't stop the drunk from his alcohol.

"Must be a dead mouse. I put out a few traps days ago and I must've nabbed one of them."

Peter wrinkled his nose and started down the steps. "Damn, you might've caught a rat by the smell of it."

Josef followed behind, staying close to Peter. He knew his window of opportunity was short. Striking while Peter was in disbelief was key. If not, there was no way he could overpower the younger man.

Five steps from the bottom.

105

Peter's boots were heavy on the wooden planks.

Four steps.

Josef could smell his sour breath over the smell of the demon.

Three steps.

In the back of his mind, Josef heard Belphegor breathing.

Two steps.

One…

"What the fuck?" Peter asked as he rounded the corner at the bottom of the steps.

Josef was right behind him, his hands poised to push Peter through the circle of protection and into the grasp of the prince demon, but he froze. It wasn't out of remorse or second thoughts, but from the sheer disgust and revulsion at seeing Belphegor again.

Runes decorated the walls, and a ring of candles flickered, and the demon stood inside the circle. The barrier was invisible, but it was solid. If it wasn't, they both would've been long dead, and God only knows what would've come.

It had been years since Josef last summoned the evil standing before him. Even in his nightmares, he didn't remember the disgust he felt, not like he did at that moment.

Belphegor stood squat and nude, surrounded by arcane wards. His body was built of terror and filth, covered with lesions and sores. Each pustule wept fluid, adding to the cornucopia of putrescence. Maggots writhed under the foreskin of the demon's flaccid penis, wriggling from crust around his glans. They fell to the ground with audible plops, many landing in the puddles of pus collecting under the beast. Short horns, appearing to have been carved from rotten wood, sprouted from his head. His nose was smushed to his face, and wet things slithered in his nostrils. A bug resembling a millipede, but not quite, fell from the demon's nose. His hellish tongue flicked out, catching the creature, before devouring it in one crunchy bite. Black fluid ran from the corners of his mouth, dripping to the floor, joining with the rest of the filth.

"Ah, finally. Some proper fucking meat!" the demon shrieked.

His voice was deep, yet piercing, more than enough to snap Josef out of his temporary fugue.

Peter had seen atrocities during the war, some of which he'd committed, but the sight of the demon was nearly too much for his mind to comprehend. It looked fake, like a fancy movie prop, but instead of being on the silver screen, it was in front of his face. Peter didn't survive all the battles in Vietnam by hesitating. He was a man of action, and he knew the beast in front of him was real—real and deadly. The voice of the beast broke his trance, igniting his fight or flight response.

"Fuck this," Peter muttered, turning to run.

Josef sensed his opportunity slipping away. He was lost in the demon's magnitude, nearly causing him to forget the reason he summoned the monstrosity.

Peter was turning. His boots were planted, and he was ready to dart up the stairs.

Josef felt like he was dipped in honey. He watched his arms snap out in front of him, lunging for Peter's chest. If he didn't get a solid purchase on the other man, there was no way he'd be able to shove him into the circle. His hands hit Peter's shoulder and chest. The hard muscle under the shirt gave Josef a start and he realized how much stronger Peter was than him. With every ounce of strength and rage Josef had, he pushed.

Peter didn't expect the attack. He'd forgotten about Josef behind him. That was, until the old man attacked him. "What the fuck?" Peter said. His feet tangled awkwardly as he turned, and stumbled backward towards the demon.

Belphegor was against the barrier. His clawed fingers were pressed against it like a pane of glass, waiting for someone to enter his lair. "Come here, meat. I'm going to rip your asshole out and eat your shit before you die," the demon growled.

Josef wanted to say something heroic, and just to Peter, to make him realize he'd done this to him, that he was going to kill him in the worst way, damning his soul to Hell to be the plaything of demons. His physical pain would be unbearable, but nothing compared to what was to come. He wanted to play the hero, but he couldn't. Josef was fighting a battle with his bladder and his shaking muscles as he tussled with Peter.

FOR THE BETTER

"Get the fuck off me," Peter said. He reached out and grabbed Josef, trying to push the older man off him, but Josef was relentless, pushing against Peter, trying to drive him back into the grasp of the demon.

Peter regained his balance and realized what Josef was trying to do; it had been his plan all along. Without warning, Peter released Josef's shirt with his right hand, and struck. His fist landed just under Josef's left eye, instantly causing the older man's grip to weaken.

Josef staggered. The blow to his face was the worst pain he'd felt in years, but he knew his job wasn't done. There was no way he could let Peter escape. His escape from the basement was a certain death for Josef, and probably for Peter's family as well.

Peter struck again, but Josef flinched, causing the blow to glance off his ear. He heard a ringing and felt pain, but the pain of failure burned even brighter.

"Get the fuck off me, you fucking kike!" Peter hissed. He pushed against Josef and loaded up for another blow.

The old man's strength was wavering, and another good punch should've been enough to break the grasp.

All at once, Peter realized why he'd been led down to the basement. He knew Josef didn't like him, that was obvious from the first time they'd met. The old man had a soft spot for Peter's family, and they had one for him, which enraged him, picking at his injured psyche. But it was then that he knew Josef knew the truth about Cindy.

"You can't have them," Peter said.

Josef grabbed his arm as he prepared to strike again. Together, the men spun, fighting for position. Each step brought them closer to the barrier holding back Belphegor.

"You killed your family. Too fucking weak to protect them, you pussy!"

Josef was losing the fight. His face hurt and his eye was swelling. Each breath came in a gasp. Soon, he'd reach his breaking point and be thrown to the demon. A part of him almost welcomed it, to die, finally, with just a glimmer of hope of seeing his family again. No, he knew Heaven wasn't for him. As much as he tried to repent, and beg for forgiveness, Josef knew he was damned—damned to spend eternity amongst creatures like Belphegor and Peter. He stumbled, almost falling to his knees.

Peter took the opportunity and shoved, knocking Josef aside.

Seeing the open staircase in front of him, Peter yanked Josef hard, trying to get him to the ground, then he let go of the old man and dashed to the stairs.

Josef was out of options. Off balance and tired, he knew the fight was over. Peter would escape and return to kill him.

As Josef's back slammed into the corner of the wall just by the staircase, he snatched at the fleeing Peter, finding purchase on his shirt. Josef pulled just hard enough to halt his escape.

He had one last option: a relic from the past, something he'd stolen from Kollmer. The Hitler youth knife shone in the dull light of the basement as Josef drew it from the sheath on his belt. It caught on his shirt as he pulled it free, but it felt good in his hand. The perverse swastika on the handle felt disgusting, but it was his only option.

"Fucker!" Peter yelled as he looked over his shoulder at Josef. His eyes went wide as the blade arched towards the back of his leg.

Sharp steel cut through dirty denim and severed the tendons behind Peter's left knee. As if they were the strings of a puppet, Peter's leg crumpled.

Josef's resolve was stronger than ever.

Blood ran down Peter's leg, soaking into the fabric of his pants.

With another yank, Josef pulled Peter off the stairs.

Peter hopped, avoiding putting any pressure on his damaged leg. In doing so, he put himself closer to the slobbering demon.

Josef released Peter's shirt, hoping the momentum would carry him into the grasp of Belphegor, but Josef wasn't that lucky. Quickly, he popped up to his feet with the blade still in his hand. He was only steps away from Peter who, again, was between him and the demon.

Violence wasn't something new to Josef and his ability to react, as opposed to think, had saved his life countless times. He knew that moment was to be one of them.

Josef struck, plunging the blade deep into Peter's gut. He expected some kind of resistance, but the blade was sharp.

Both men looked down at the handle protruding from Peter's stomach. Their faces were mirrors of shock, but Josef, again, was quicker. He yanked the blade out of Peter's belly and thrust again. This time, Peter's instincts took over. He stepped back and reached down to stop the knife from violating him further, and his leg, the one with the severed tendons, buckled. The stumble cost him his life.

Josef's aim was true. The blade entered Peter's ribs.

"Yes! Yes!" Belphegor screamed. Black putrescence ran down the invisible barrier as he spat with every word. More bugs skittered out of his wounds. Many fell from his widening urethra before they were squashed under his feet.

Peter was on the cusp of the barrier. The knife was wedged between his ribs, and a steady flow of blood dripped from the injuries he sustained.

Josef still had the handle of the weapon, but it was stuck. He knew this was his last chance.

Something changed in Peter's face. Fear, almost childlike, washed over him. His jeans darkened as his bladder released just a moment before the back of his skull entered the barrier.

Belphegor was like a lion in a cage: hungry and ready to feed. He grabbed Peter's head as soon as it entered his domain, and pulled. Claws wrapped over top of Peter's face, plunging into his eyes. Grotesque nails popped the soft orbs as Peter screamed and fought.

Peter grabbed at the demon's hands and pulled, but it was like a child fighting an adult, like Cindy having a chance against her drunken, abusive father.

With his free hand, Belphegor grabbed Peter's left arm and twisted. The bones snapped, and a squirt of blood from Peter's shredded brachial artery dripped down the barrier.

Peter's mouth opened wider to scream, but the demon was ready.

Belphegor released the shattered arm and grabbed Peter's lower jaw. His other hand was still buried in the doomed man's ocular cavity, and with a quick yank, he pulled Peter's head apart with a snap akin to cracking crab legs.

Josef watched. He watched as the demon ripped the corpse to pieces, shoving bone, meat, and dripping viscera into its filthy mouth. He watched as pieces of a man who'd been alive and breathing only moments before were turned to meat. Each time he sacrificed someone to the monster, Josef felt just a touch of remorse that he could so easily take a life, regardless of how evil that person was.

Belphegor was crouched over the pile of mush and denim that had once been Peter when he saw Josef grab the holy water. "So soon?" the demon grumbled. A finger was wedged in his teeth. "I was hoping you'd have more meat for me. It's been ages since you've fed me, Jew. You're not looking too good." The demon smiled. "One day you will die and then you'll be mine. My brothers and I will eat you and fuck you for eternity."

Josef's gorge rose. His throat burned from the bile. Demons were masters of lies and deception, but he knew Belphegor spoke the truth. Josef wasn't getting any younger. Each day that ticked by was one day closer to the grave and into the clutches of the underworld. He hoped the death of Peter bought him some more time, but how much, he wasn't certain.

Josef couldn't live like that—trading lives to prolong his. He told himself that, but when death came knocking, could he keep his word? That was a question he'd ask himself another day.

He splashed the holy water onto the blistered skin of Belphegor. It popped and hissed.

The demon smiled as it deformed and headed back into the stone. "One day, Jew. One day, you'll be mine, just like your wife and kids," Belphegor said as his body morphed, losing its form. Then, he was sucked into the rock once again and everything went silent.

Josef shuddered. He dropped the empty container of holy water to the basement floor.

FOR THE BETTER

Slowly, he sat on the stairs, put his face in his hands, and wept.

Chapter 8

Snow whipped around the street, dancing along the curb in a flurry of wild abandon. Josef stared out the window like he'd done so many times over the years. His eyes weren't locked on the flurries, but on the moving truck parked across the street.

Months had gone by since Josef lured Peter into the basement. The first few days after had been tough, especially once the police arrived. Janet, seeing her husband's truck parked in the driveway, had worried. Josef didn't know if she was concerned about where he was or where he *might be*, like a hiding monster waiting to jump out and get you.

The police came and knocked on everyone's doors, Josef's included. It was more of a formality than anything, but it was still their job.

Everyone expected the day to come when either Peter or Janet would up and leave. It turned out Peter was the first to do it, at least to the layman.

Josef feigned concern, sticking to the script he'd come to in his head. He told them how terrible it was that a man could just leave his wife and daughter, especially a daughter who was in a coma.

The detectives jotted a few notes, accompanied by some disinterested grunts, and left Josef alone. No one suspected any foul play and if they did, it certainly wasn't directed at the old man.

Janet had spent many days at Josef's house, a whirlwind of emotions running through her. She wept on his shoulder, scared for the future of her daughter.

Cindy had made little improvement, but there was some, enough to give her hope.

And Janet cried for Peter.

Josef hadn't, and would never tell her the truth, but he cradled her and let her weep. Deep down, he knew her tears were full of mixed emotions. She was upset, but not for the lack of companionship. No, she was worried about money. Peter's job wasn't the best, but it was enough to keep the lights on and a roof over their heads. With him gone, disappearing into the ether, Janet didn't know what to do. Their savings were almost non-existent, with most of that going towards hospital bills for Cindy. Peter had a small life insurance policy given to him by his uncle when he was a boy, but without a death certificate, Janet had no chance of collecting. In the long run, she knew she was in trouble, and so did Josef.

With the deaths of the Nazis, Josef didn't have to witness the aftermath of his actions. He never had to see a grieving family or console a widow. He killed them without remorse or thought of repercussion, but watching the movers load the truck, he was feeling the weight of his decision.

Janet opened the trunk of her car—the one she'd bought after selling Peter's truck—and set down a suitcase. A bitter wind pulled at the scarf around her neck, but she kept her collar closed against the torrent.

Someone else came down the driveway, and Josef lit up with glee.

Cindy hobbled along, still feeling the effects of her recovery, but she was alive. Not only was she alive, but she was well. The damage to her brain healed almost completely, leaving her with just the slightest of limp, and according to the doctors, that would eventually fade. She made a miraculous recovery like none of them had ever seen.

Josef felt the sting of tears in his eyes watching the girl. His aches and pains were still there, but not as deep as they used to be, not since the night with the demon. He didn't know how the evil deals were made, or who received the blessing (curse?) of the demon, but it felt as if he and Cindy shared it that time, and for that, he was grateful. If he had a choice, Josef would've given her the entirety of it.

Cindy looked across the street as if she could feel his gaze upon her.

Josef raised his hand as they locked eyes. He gave her a little wave.

Cindy smiled at him and returned the gesture. She turned to Janet and spoke, then Janet looked across to him and waved, and then said something to Cindy.

Without hesitation, Cindy made her way towards him.

Josef, seeing the difficulty with which the girl walked, quickly put on a pair of boots and grabbed his coat, rushing out into the snow. Bitter wind, and sharp flakes snapped at his face, but he didn't care. Seeing the smile on Cindy's face warmed him more than enough to brave the cold. He wasn't the fastest man, but he was quicker than an injured little girl.

"My my, it's nice to see you up and moving again," he said.

Cindy had stopped at the edge of her yard, leaning against the mailbox. Her cheeks were red, but her eyes were full of wonder and life, something Josef didn't know if he'd ever see again. "Yeah, I'm still kinda sore, but the doctors told me that could happen. I get dizzy if I move too much, but it should go away in a few months, I hope," she said with a smile.

Josef smiled too, but could feel the familiar sting of tears burning. This was 'goodbye,' and he knew it. There might be the occasional letter or phone call in the next few days or weeks, but they'd dwindle, and one day he'd realize he hadn't heard from Cindy or Janet in a few months. He'd try to call the number he had for them, but it would be disconnected. Every letter he'd send would be returned unopened. Once again, Josef would be left in the grips of loneliness, forced to wallow in the silence of an empty house.

An *almost* empty house.

He wanted to look back at the windows of the living room, but he didn't; he knew the demon was locked away in the stone. In that instance, if he turned, he knew Belphegor would be watching. No matter what, he could always *feel* him watching.

"Well, that's certainly good to hear," Josef said. He reached out and rubbed her shoulder.

Cindy's eyes averted, looking down at the snow as it grew in the roadway. "I...I just don't know why..." she started, but a sob wracked her frail body.

Josef stepped forward and took her in his arms, letting her collapse into him. His tears, which he'd been fighting back, rushed out. "Shhh." His cheek was pressed against the top of Cindy's head, his tears wetting her hair. Gently, he rubbed her back, doing his best to console the girl.

He didn't know if the day would ever come, but he knew he couldn't lie to her, not completely. "Your daddy was a sick man, a very sick man, but it wasn't his fault. War can change a person, I know."

Cindy's tears and sobs came harder.

"But I can tell you this," Josef took a step back, willing the girl to lift her face from his chest.

Cindy looked up at him, keeping her cries under control, but allowing the tears to fall. There was fear in her eyes. A fear of something she and her mother both knew but would never say aloud: her father was gone, and not just that he skipped town; he was gone for good.

"Your father will *never* hurt you or your mother again." Josef's voice wavered, but he got it out.

Janet tossed a last bag into the car and watched them. The car purred, and a cloud of exhaust rose into the air. Slowly, she made her way over to them.

Josef stared at Cindy, letting his gaze and her's lock. Something flashed in her eyes. It was a brief look of sadness that was washed away by a mixture of relief and optimism. She knew that was the first day of the rest of her life, that she and her mother were free of her father. And some days may hurt more than others, but deep down, they knew life would change for the better without him.

"Hey, what's with all the crying over here?" Janet asked. Her nose was red, but her eyes were wide and full. She looked at Josef and Cindy, who were still in a semi-embrace.

Josef let the girl go, helping her grab back on to the mailbox for support. "Oh, you know, goodbyes are always hard," Josef said. He wiped his eyes with the back of his hand.

Janet stepped forward and hugged him. She planted a warm kiss on his cold cheek. "This is just goodbye for now. I'll be sure to call you and send you all of our information once we get settled."

Josef just nodded, knowing his voice would betray him. His chest hurt from holding back the sobs. He pulled Janet in for a final hug; her lips nearly touching his ears.

"Thank you, Josef," she whispered.

Josef didn't respond, there was no need to.

FOR THE BETTER

"Ma'am, we need to get going before the snow gets much worse," one of the movers said. He was a burly guy, tall and strong, with a belly that pressed against his jumpsuit.

The big truck was loaded and secured, ready to usher the Ward women into their new future.

The snowstorm had gone from a squall to a full-on blizzard. Josef felt the cold in his bones as he wrapped his rejuvenated body in a thick robe. His slippered feet shuffled into the kitchen and he set up the coffee pot. The steady dripping echoed in the quiet house, filling the dead space with a heavenly smell. School had been canceled, which he knew the night before. He had a stack of papers to grade, and the day off would allow him the reprieve he needed to let his red pencil work.

A heavy thump rattled the front door. Bright white shone through the window. The early sunlight reflected off the fresh blanket of snow. It was supposed to be a record snowfall and with luck, school would be canceled the next day as well, taking him right into the weekend.

Josef opened the door, looking at the winter wonderland in his front yard. Resting on top of the snow was his morning paper.

The paperboy struggled through the street, sliding on the fresh powder.

The street—besides the grunting of the paperboy—was quiet. In the distance, a train horn blared. The cold air carried the sound over the snow, and into Josef's ears. His mind snapped back to the platform in Auschwitz—the last place he saw his family.

Family.

It still amazed him that men like Peter could exist. To have a loving wife and a child you created, yet be so hateful. How could men be so similar and different at the same time? It was a thought that had plagued Josef's mind for decades. How could people like the Nazis and Peter exist in a civilized world? No matter how far along humanity progressed, there would always be evil. But faced with evil, there stood those that were just.

Josef didn't know where he stood. He was a killer. He took life like he was God. Acting as judge, jury, and executioner, Josef took the most basic freedom of life from people, and he knew he'd do it again. Deep down, he knew every man he'd killed was a monster, a taker of lives themselves, and deserving of death. But who was he to decide? When death finally came for him, how would he be judged? As a monster or an angel?

A bitter wind blew, whipping a flurry of snow into his face. Josef clutched the paper to his chest and pulled his robe tight.

The Ward house sat alone. A thin wisp of smoke curled up from the chimney. He knew no one was home, but he could wish.

FOR THE BETTER

He stared at the front door, the one with the key box hanging from the knob. He held his breath, as if waiting for Cindy to come rushing into the whiteness, bundled up with a sled in her hands. She'd pile snow in the front yard using an old shovel and ride down that little hill until her nose was the color of a beet.

The door remained closed. And the house—for the meantime—was vacant. But Josef knew something else lived in there—memories: ghosts of pain and sleepless nights leading to fearful mornings. Janet's fear of invoking the ire of her husband as he stumbled in drunk, looking at her with lustfully abusive eyes, or worse, the pain Cindy felt from his fists, of hearing her mother whimper or cry as the bed groaned in protest at the violations.

Another sharp gust and Josef jumped as his door blew completely open, slamming into the wall. Realizing his toes were wet and numb, he shook off the trance and walked back. The warmth of the house was inviting, but the smell of the coffee was even better. He kicked off his slippers, knowing he'd need to put them in the dryer, and walked barefoot into the kitchen.

He grabbed a mug, filled it with hot, black coffee, and pulled the paper from the plastic. If Josef hadn't been positioned over a chair, he would've hit the floor. His behind hit the wood, and hot coffee splashed on his cold hand. He hardly noticed the scalding as his eyes scanned the text below the horrific picture.

The front page of the paper was chaos. Overnight, a massive pileup involving dozens of cars occurred on the interstate. Tractor trailers, snowplows, and passenger vehicles were all involved.

"…numerous injuries, some life-threatening," Josef read aloud. "Thousands of dollars' worth of damage." He swallowed the hard lump in his throat. "Two confirmed fatalities. A vehicle was struck from behind, causing the gas tank to ignite. The occupants of the vehicle have yet to be identified due to the horrific nature of their burns. An autopsy will be conducted, and dental records examined to learn the identity of the unfortunate travelers…" his voice trailed off.

Josef's eyes stung. It couldn't be them. The world wasn't that cruel to let them out of the pot and into the fire. But then again, the world allowed millions to be slaughtered. A low sob escaped his lips and tears ran down his face. He told himself it wasn't them; they wouldn't have been on that stretch of the interstate. They should've been at their new place by then. Josef lied to himself, doing what he could to ignore the inevitable. His cries intensified.

"Fuck you!" He snapped his head up and backhanded the coffee cup, shattering it against the counter.

Outside, the wind howled through the branches. A howl that sounded like laughter.

FOR THE BETTER

3rd, September 1993

I'm dying.

It's been 22 years since I've opened this book. Another long stretch of time where it's sat forgotten, dust-covered. A long time since I've had much to write about. And since my last entry was about the Ward family, this hasn't been the most enjoyable moment of my life. A life I know is ending.

Until now, things have been good—as good as they can be, I suppose. That is, until a week ago. My stomach has always been solid, allowing me to eat whatever I'd like. Nothing bothers me, and even as a boy, I could eat and not have issues. The night the cramps came, I'd figured it was just a bout of indigestion. I didn't realize it at first, but I'm now in my early nineties, so it's not out of the realm of possibility that food would bother me. Even with the tainted gift of the demon, my body has continued to age. Albeit at a much slower pace. I may be ninety-something, but anyone would be hard-pressed to even put me into my seventies.

The cramping stuck with me throughout the night and when I woke, I had to rush to the toilet. Embarrassed, even alone, I almost didn't make it in time. I've had dysentery, parasites, and many bouts of food poisoning, so diarrhea was familiar to me. What came out of me that day was far from familiar.

Blood. The toilet was slick with greasy stool and blood. I nearly fainted at the sight of it but held it together. Another cramp tore through my guts, and

127

luckily, I was still on the bowl. My insides felt full of liquid fire as more poured from me. I cleaned myself, rinsed my face with cold water and took long, deep breaths.

My doctor, a young seventy-five-year-old (young to me, at least) told me it was probably nothing, but I could see the worry on his face. I know my results will be in soon, and I feel as if I'm waiting for death to call my name. As if I'm back in the camps with a gun pointed at my head, staring into the pit of a mass grave just waiting for the bullet to enter my skull.

I'm not a stupid man. I know my body and even with what I've been gifted, know this will probably be the end of me. It is something I've looked forward to, yet dreaded for decades. Death scares me not. If the sweet embrace of finality will grant me time with my Ola and the boys once again, then let it come. But what if it doesn't? I know now there's a Hell. And sadly, I know what beasts dwell below. Will the men I've killed be there to welcome me at the left hand of Satan?

Never again. It's a promise I made the day after I killed Peter Ward. But now that I may be standing at the crossroads of death, is that a promise I can keep? What will become of the demon when I'm gone? Who can I give it to, and what burden would I leave them? Would it be for the better if I bury the stone or cast it into the sea? But what then? Maybe that won't be the end. That might only delay the inevitable of someone else finding it. Or worse yet, somehow setting Belphegor free. Besides, I know it's for naught. The stone—the demon—is linked to me now. I could drive to the sea and cast it deep, and I know it will be waiting for me when I return.

I am the only one that can keep him at bay. To keep the monster hidden and locked away.

Sick. I'm a sick man. Yes, sick in the physical sense. But I'm sick in my mind. I know it. To keep the monster hidden and safe, I need to be around. To be alive and aware of myself. And what I have growing in my guts will see me dead in months, if not weeks. I am sick because I know what I must do.

Animal sacrifices won't work. They might have helped keep Schatzi around, but at my age and health, it would do nothing for me. Possibly granting me a day or so, but what is that in the grand scheme of life?

A person. It has to be another person. It is unthinkable to kill again, but what can I do? Leave this monster behind, hoping it isn't released?

I am sick.

I just wish this would all end.

CHAPTER 9

The warmth of summer wasn't going anywhere. Rays of bright sun baked the campus, tanning the exposed flesh of the students as they walked to class.

Josef, despite the warm weather, was cold. It was a chill that didn't come from the air, but from within. Ever since the day he saw Doctor Gosko, a ball of ice seemed to live in his gut. He didn't know if it was part of his sickness, or if it was the feeling of impending doom.

The college was larger than the one where he'd previously taught. This was a nice change, and took him out of Manhattan. It wasn't a massive school, just big enough to make walking across campus annoying. Normally, Josef wouldn't mind the walk, it had been part of his routine for years, especially when Schatzi was alive. Just like he'd never remarried, Josef never owned another dog. He couldn't bear it again—the loss of another companion, or the lengths at which he'd go to keep them around. There were some nights when he could hear the screams of the stray dog he fed to the demon to keep his Schatzi alive.

Since he felt like he'd swallowed a ball of ice, and the pain in his gut, Josef loathed having to walk. Hunched and with damp armpits of cold sweat, he walked into his classroom.

The new year had just started, and the students were eager to learn. It was always short-lived. As an educator for half a century, Josef knew the routine.

Students began filtering into the classroom, and with them walked Josef's dead wife, Ola.

Josef dropped the folder he was holding. His heart skipped a beat, and for a moment, he didn't think it would start again. Pain like a fist squeezing his chest crushed him. *This is it,* he thought. He braced himself on the desk, but kept looking at Ola. His heart thumped and thumped, resuming its normal rhythm.

The pain left as quickly as it had come. Josef expected Ola to leave as well, drifting away like the apparition she was. But she didn't.

She turned, and Josef shuddered. It wasn't his wife; it was a student. She was almost perfect. Her body was identical to his late wife's, and her hair was the right shade. If it weren't for the newer style and the slight upturn to the girl's nose, she would've been identical.

"Are you okay?" someone asked.

Josef realized he was sweating even worse than when he'd walked into the classroom. He didn't have a mirror, but knew he looked terrible. It was just a feeling, like he'd eaten rotten food filled with bugs—bugs like those that made their homes in the putrid flesh of Belphegor.

Josef stood tall, cleared his throat, and turned to the speaker.

FOR THE BETTER

A young man with a smattering of acne on his cheeks and a pair of glasses perched on his nose, looked at him.

"Yes, yes," Josef said. "I'm fine." He put on a smile. "Even us old goats can get first-day jitters."

The boy smiled back at the aging professor and drifted in amongst his classmates.

Soon, they were seated, and their chatter died down. All eyes were on Josef, but his eyes kept wandering to the girl who looked like his wife.

He turned his back to the class and picked up a fresh piece of chalk, then wrote his name on the board and turned back to the room. "Good morning, I'm Mr. Lazerowitz."

Her name was Brenda Fahnstock, and she'd been on Josef's mind since the first period of the day. Even as he drove to his doctor's appointment, he couldn't help but think of the girl. Her resemblance to his wife was uncanny at best, but Josef couldn't help but think of her as a sign.

There wasn't much one-on-one talk in college, especially on the first day. Most students were just as eager to end their day as the teachers, and when the bell rang, they'd be off to their next class.

Throughout the lesson, Josef and Brenda made eye contact. It was like staring at Ola, and a few times he had to stop himself from calling her by his dead wife's name.

Brenda was attentive, listening to him, and taking notes. Even as he droned on, she hung on his words.

Having her in class was the distraction he needed leading up to his appointment. When he pulled into the parking lot of the medical building, Josef's mind went back to reality and the pain in his gut, not the flutter in his heart.

The office was small, and the nurse brought him right into an exam room. "The doctor will be with you in just a second," she said.

The look in her eyes was not one of hope. It was the same look he'd seen in the eyes of prisoners when they realized one of their fellows would die. Whether it was from a disease, or a gunshot, they knew death was coming.

Josef smiled, but it was forced. The door clicked as loudly as the lump in his throat.

The room was small and cold. He sat on the exam table, with the sanitary paper crinkling underneath him, looking at the posters on the walls.

Living with cancer: How to make the best of your time.

Chemo: Fight back with the treatment of the future.

Prepping for surgery: How to prepare your mind, body, and spirit.

What's wrong with me?: How to explain cancer to a child.

FOR THE BETTER

The doorknob jiggled, and Josef snapped his eyes from the literature.

Doctor Gosko walked in, holding a folder in his hands. "Good afternoon," he said, and pulled a stool from under the desk and sat down. His belly pushed against his white coat as he set the folder down on his knees.

"Is it?" Josef asked.

The doctor looked at him, surprised.

Even Josef felt the shock of surprise, as he wasn't planning to say that.

Gosko's lips twitched, making his gray mustache dance. He took his glasses off as if to see his patient better. "No, no it's not."

Right to the chase. Good, thought Josef. *I'm too damn old to beat around the bush.* "Just tell me."

Gosko opened Josef's chart. "Cancer, Mr. Lazerowitz." He took a few pieces of paper out with a slew of medical terms typed all over them. "Stage four."

Josef nodded. It was what he'd expected, but hearing it made it real. Too real. "What are my options?" It was a stupid question. He damn well knew his options. Chemo, infusions, maybe surgery. All of them were shit. Just more money and more pain, and in the end, he'd die, and die horribly.

He knew the only *real* option if he wanted to live, but he didn't know if the price was worth his life, or better yet, his soul.

The doctor removed a few pamphlets from the folder, along with some more forms. He blathered on about treatment and the effects of chemo. "I can give you these to help with the pain." With a script only legible by doctors and pharmacists, Gosko scrawled down a prescription.

Josef took the piece of paper handed to him, hardly listening. Instead, he nodded when he needed to. His mind wasn't in the room; it was in his basement. It was with the demon, Belphegor, the only *true* treatment to what ailed him.

Chapter 10

Josef fell into a fitful sleep. The pain in his stomach subsided, but still lurked in the depths of his body. Every time he moved, a tremor of burning pain ran through his gut. He considered taking the pills, but part of him felt as if the pain was his penance. It wasn't the easiest way to fall asleep, but somehow, he did.

His classroom was all set, as it was earlier in the day. Bright-eyed students sat staring, and he smiled back at them. He felt good, young and spry, like a man half his age. Josef grabbed his chalk and turned his back to the class, writing on the board.

"So, today, we'll begin our lesson on Freud. Now, I'm sure most of you—" he spun back to face them and stopped.

The classroom was empty and dim. Only a few lights burned above, showing the darkened rows of seats. Josef squinted into the gloom but saw nothing.

"Okay, very funny." He set the chalk down and dusted off his hands. "Turn the lights back on and let's get on with the lesson."

The lights remained dim, but something moved in the darkness. Something—no, someone—came from the shadows. A familiar smell accompanied the newcomer, sending Josef's heart fluttering.

"Ola?"

The sweetness of her perfume ushered her into the classroom.

"Ola!" Josef yelled, rushing from behind his desk as she came into the light. But something was wrong. He paused and stared at the woman in front of him. "Brenda?"

Brenda smiled. Even that looked like Josef's dead wife. "Hello, Professor."

"W…what are you doing here? Class is over." Josef looked confused. "I'm sorry. I thought you were someone else."

Brenda walked closer to him. Her shirt was snug, and her nipples pressed against the fabric, pulling his eyes towards them. "I know, but she's dead and gone, turned to ash in an incinerator in Poland. But you have me." She stepped closer, within arm's reach. Brenda placed her hand on Josef's chest.

The feeling was electric. Josef shuddered at her touch. Even that reminded him of Ola. His blood pumped, rushing heat around his body. Something stirred in his pants, and an erection—a sensation not felt in decades—grew.

Brenda smiled at him, knowing of his arousal. Her left hand reached down and stroked his swollen member. "I see your body still remembers."

Josef closed his eyes. It wasn't his wife, and yet his body was betraying him. Many years had passed since he'd felt a woman's touch. Brenda wasn't Ola, but he could imagine it, he had to. He missed her so much it was painful. Even though it felt wrong to want the younger woman, it felt right.

A light kiss touched Josef's agape mouth. It was a taste he would recognize anywhere and anytime.

Ola.

"Josef, kiss me," Ola said.

Josef's eyes flickered open. Before him stood his wife. Not the spry, young co-ed lookalike, but his wife. His Ola.

"Ola!" he said, wrapping her in his arms.

They kissed long and deeply. Tears mixed with saliva and their loins stirred with long-lost excitement.

Ola backed away from him, breaking the kiss. Her rump hit the desk, and she pushed herself up onto it. "Make love to me," she said as she spread her legs. The hem of her dress fell to her waist as she raised her knees.

Josef, without touching his pants, stood nude. His erection bobbed in front of him, aimed at his wife's exposed sex like a divining rod. He crawled onto the desk and plunged into her.

Electric. That was the only word flashing through his mind. Josef fell on her, letting Ola's breath tickle his neck. He cried as he thrust, so happy to be in the embrace of his wife once again.

Ola's arms wrapped around his neck. Her lips touched his ear.

"How does that feel, Loverboy?" asked Belphegor.

Josef pulled away from his wife's arms and looked down. Ola stared back at him, but something was amiss. It was subtle, but it was there. *Her eyes!* he thought. *Something is wrong with her eyes.*

Ola stared at him with blackness. Her once beautiful eyes were the color of coal. Something moved under her flesh, creeping towards her tear duct.

Josef, realizing he was still inside of her, pulled back, but was stuck.

"Where are you going, Jew?" the demon asked. The taint of his voice coming from the beautiful mouth of Ola was an affront to God.

The wriggling under her skin grew like the surface of a disturbed pond. Tiny legs appeared at the corner of Ola's eyes. Clawed appendages grabbed at the slick orb, creating little drops of blood as it crawled its way out.

"No!" Josef screamed, again trying to pull out of his wife.

"Yes!" Belphegor yelled.

Bugs flew from Ola's mouth. They were wet, covered in congealed blood and gore. A bubble of filth popped and covered Ola's face in tar-like putrescence. More bugs crawled out of the thin flesh around her eyes, biting and clawing the dark orbs.

Josef pulled once again, and this time, he was freed. He landed hard on his ass, making his teeth click.

Ola stood. She was an effigy of rot. With clawed fingers, she ripped her dress apart. Long rents of blood glistened on her shredded flesh, new openings to allow more rot to pour forth.

"Mr. Lazer, what's going on?"

Josef's head snapped to the side, seeing Brenda.

"What the fuck is that?" She pointed at the creature that was once his wife.

Josef looked at Ola, but she was gone. Her mutilated corpse was in the hands of Belphegor, who stood in her place.

The demon, standing taller than ever, held Ola's nude body in his hands. Her head lolled to the side, dead. A black centipede, the thickness of Josef's thumb, crawled from her mouth. It fell to the floor with a wet plop and skittered towards him.

"Mmm, this is fine meat, Jew," Belphegor said. He plunged his face into Ola's gut, ripping at the soft flesh of her belly. Blood and entrails dripped from the demon's mouth as he chewed, staring at Josef. "But nothing is as good as cunt-meat." Belphegor spun Ola's body so her vagina was facing his mouth. He opened wide and clamped his jaws over her sex, biting through flesh and bone.

"Soon, I'll eat the little worm you call a cock." Bits of Ola fell from the demon's mouth as it spoke.

"Josef," Brenda said. Her breath tickled his ear.

His head snapped to the side. The mutilated face of the girl stared back at him. Her mouth was open, and smoke flowed from it—smoke with the scent of almonds.

Zyklon-B. He thought back to the death-gas favored by the Nazis. The scent was something he'd never forget.

Josef's mouth opened, breathing in the fumes. "I…I ah…" the words fell from his lips like the descent of corpses into a mass grave. Hot fire tore into his stomach. With his breath caught in his throat and the stench of Zyklon in his nose, Josef looked down. The hand of Belphegor protruded from just above his belly button, and warm blood ran down his nude body, coating his flaccid penis in gore.

"There is a disease inside of you," Belphegor growled. "It's eating you from the inside out. I can take it away, give it to someone else, maybe a child. Maybe I'll just eat it, savoring your pain. But, you know if I do not help you, you will die, Jew. You will die covered in your stinking shit and blood, crying, not for the pain of your flesh, but for your soul. And once the life leaves you, you are mine."

Josef couldn't breathe. He stared at Brenda, who looked back at him with corpse eyes. Pain pulled at his gut, ripping through him.

Brenda opened her mouth and Zyklon-B poured out. "You know what you need to do."

Josef found his lungs, breathing the gas in deep, and screamed.

Chapter 11

Josef was wet.

He awoke screaming, pulling at the covers over him. A stench assaulted his nostrils and for a moment, he thought he was still in the nightmare. But no, it was reality. Josef's shaking fingers found the lamp next to his bed. The warmth of the filth was dissipating as cold seeped in. The dim light of the bulb cast a yellow glow in the room. He threw the covers back, knowing what he'd find.

Bloody shit leaked through his pajamas.

He sprung out of bed, leaving a grotesque stain behind. The thin pants stuck to his shivering body. Filth ran down his legs and Josef did his best to dart to the bathroom.

Core memories—memories of the camp—came back to him. The smell of spilled shit, the fear and shame felt by prisoners fresh from the train trying to maintain some semblance of dignity. In the end, no amount of dignity could save them. They all died the same way: screaming and clawing the walls to escape the gas.

Josef climbed into the shower, but left the water off. He peeled the tacky pants from his withered body. The smell of his excrement was bad enough, but seeing the blood was something different. His death was coming, and coming fast. It was inevitable, but the words of the demon made his fear even more real.

When nude, Josef turned the water on. He didn't give it a chance to warm up. The shock and discomfort of the cold water was his penance. It was the punishment for something he'd not even done, but worried he would.

A slurry of watery feces mixed with blood ran down the drain. Together, it mixed with his tears.

There was no point in going back to bed. With the sheets stripped and his pajamas in the trash, Josef sat at his kitchen table. It was still dark, and the oven clock taunted him with its green numbers, showing it was 4:12 in the morning.

Josef wanted a cup of coffee, but his stomach revolted at just the thought of it, so he settled for tea instead. The mug steamed in front of him. His hands were wrapped around it, attempting to steal the chill from his body. Slowly, he raised it to his lips, sipping. The tea burned the entire way down, but Josef sipped deeper, relishing the heat.

Josef looked at nothing, and yet, saw everything; a thousand-yard stare is what most people called it. His eyes were locked on the wall, but they didn't see the garish paper. Instead, they saw the finality of his life: the end he would soon suffer, and what would come from that. They saw the demon in the hands of evil, or even worse, unleashed and uncontrolled.

His watery eyes also saw a way out. Not a cure, but a solution to delay the inevitable. He would die, that was for certain, but he didn't have to die yet. Josef knew that, but didn't know if he had it in him to make the move. Part of him wanted to pull the bandage off and yank, letting the cancer eat him alive, leaving him dead and at the mercy of God. But fear held him tight, and since the day he'd been cursed with Belphegor, it wasn't a fear of the unknown, but of the *known*.

Josef dumped the remaining tea into the sink, bag and all. He rinsed the cup and set it down on the drying rack.

It was early, but he knew some people would be out. They always were. He wouldn't act, just look. *But why bother looking if you're not going to do it?* he asked himself. *I won't do it. It's just an option if I decide to change my mind.*

Your mind is made up, Pet Jew, Belphegor growled from the recesses of Josef's mind.

He shivered and felt a blade of pain in his guts. Cold sweat coated his skin, but the pain left as quickly as it came. Without another thought, he grabbed his keys and darted out into the gloom of the early morning.

The Myers was a part of town where Josef rarely ventured. As he drove through the dim neighborhood, he couldn't remember an actual time of being there. He'd seen the rundown section of the city from the highway, but that was about it. Most people were scared to tread in The Myers, but Josef knew true evil. Fear was something so deeply ingrained in his psyche, that a mugger or carjacking was the least of his concerns.

The derelict neighborhood was a scene that could've been pulled from any metropolitan area. Check cashing, pawn shops, liquor stores, gun stores, gas stations, and fast food lined the streets. Trash littered the sidewalk, caught in the storm drain. Roll doors were down and locked tight, many covered in various graffiti. A few people wandered the street, most picking through the garbage either looking for cans to cash in or a meal.

Josef drove slowly. His car wasn't the newest, but it stood out against the few vehicles on the road. Traffic was light, but more than a few cars rolled down the side streets. He hit his blinker and turned, narrowly avoiding a mangy stray dog.

Thoughts of Schatzi and the stray he'd sacrificed for her life, came back to him. But he wasn't down in The Myers looking for stray animals. He was looking for stray people, and from the chatter of his co-workers and students, Josef knew exactly where to look.

Chamber Street was notorious for whores. Josef didn't know why, as it looked like every other street in The Myers, but it was. Maybe it was the lack of streetlights or proximity to the highway, but either way, the street—even at 4 a.m.—had women walking it.

Josef drove, ashamed to look at the exposed skin of the women. The summer heat kept the night warm, and the ladies of Chamber Street were on full display.

Pockmarked faces, looking aged and weathered, smiled at him through masks of makeup. Stuffed bras sat lumpy against breasts withered away from years of addiction. Fresh scabs in the crooks of elbows were a tell-tale sign of intravenous drug use.

Josef left his windows up. The cat-calls from the girls could still be heard through the glass, but not clearly; it sounded as if they were under water. He felt like he was drowning as he looked at each girl he passed. A few of them were young, *very* young. He didn't pray for them and wouldn't—it was pointless.

The headlights of his car hit the face of a girl no older than twenty. Josef slowed the car, but didn't stop completely. Under the right conditions, the girl could've passed for a strung-out version of Brenda. She didn't look too much like the healthy co-ed, but something in her eyes made Josef shiver with recognition. He didn't think she could see him well, but the girl looked at him through the windshield and smiled.

She raised a dirty hand in a wave, blocking out his headlights. Her face was made-up and bore the look of defeat. The joy in her fake smile never reached her eyes.

Slowly, Josef rolled towards her. Without thinking, he rolled down the window as the defeated girl walked up to his car.

"How's it going?" she asked. A smell of cheap perfume, cigarettes, and body odor wafted into the car.

Josef shuddered. *Leave! Drive away and don't come back!* he screamed at himself. *Don't do this.*

Josef sat frozen with his foot on the brake pedal, but itched to press the accelerator, "I…ah…"

The girl looked at him with a touch of caring in her eyes, like he was a wounded dog.

Josef was sure he wasn't the first elderly widower to drive those streets.

"Are you looking for some company?" She leaned over, giving Josef a glimpse of her cleavage.

No, I'm looking for someone no one will miss that I can feed to a fucking demon to make myself healthy so I don't wake up covered in my shit again, he thought. "I'm sorry," Josef said. A little faster than expected, he lifted his foot off the brake and hit the gas.

The girl moved her arms just in time as Josef sped away in the pinkness of dawn's light.

CHAPTER 12

A gaunt, sallow-looking man stared at Josef in the mirror. His cheeks were sunken and his eyes had a corona of darkness.

It had been a week since Josef ventured into The Myers, a week of short nights and long days of torment and fear of not making it to the toilet in time. And just moments earlier, it was one of those times. As he was mid-lecture, a lance of white-hot pain tore through his stomach.

An internal countdown began, one where Josef knew he needed a toilet and quickly. He hunched and used his podium to keep himself up, but he could hear the murmur of the students. Most were remarks about his health, but some were snide and rude.

The bell rang, and it was the sound of freedom. Without a word, Josef shuffled out of the classroom, and clenched the entire way to the toilet.

He wiped his face with a damp paper towel, then re-wet it and wiped the back of his sweaty neck. The sound of his watch ticking was loud in his throbbing brain. There was only one class left and he hoped he could make it. That had been his fourth panicked shit of the day, not including the one he took before leaving the house. Each movement became looser and looser, containing more blood.

His appetite was gone; the primary source of his sustenance was thin soup. Each time he waited

149

for his meal, he thought of the soup he ate in Auschwitz, how each man would try to be towards the end of the line, praying to get some chunks in their bowl. But then again, such a move could be risky. If they ran out of soup, the prisoners that were at the end wouldn't eat until the evening.

Another countdown had also begun in Josef's mind: the ticking clock of mortality. Josef didn't know how much time he had left, but he knew it wasn't long. He'd ignored the repeated calls from the doctor, knowing the man couldn't help him. Even if Josef went with a more 'traditional' method, he was too far gone to save. The only thing he could do was to postpone the inevitable, but not for long.

Josef took a deep breath, doing his best to fight back tears. He knew what he had to do; he only hoped he was strong enough to do it.

Josef made it through his last class without an issue, he even felt slightly better than he had before the day started. He wasn't sure if it was a fluke or the surge of energy a doomed individual feels before death. Whatever it was, he was grateful.

The day was another beautiful one. Josef parked as close as he could to the building, but still had a bit of a walk. He didn't exactly have a skip in his step, but he was no longer doubled over in pain.

"Mr. Lazer," someone said.

Josef slowed and stopped, looking for the owner of the voice. A few groups of students walked, but one girl cut loose from the crowd.

Brenda.

Ola.

Even though he knew his wife was dead and gone, he couldn't help but see her in the young woman. But, in Brenda, he saw the prostitute, the one with a look of despair and dead stars of hope in her eyes.

"Oh, yes, hello," he said, feeling clumsy.

Brenda stopped in front of him and looked down at her feet. "Are you okay?" She was blunt.

Josef forced a smile. He hadn't been that close to her and the resemblance to Ola was staggering. A flash of shame washed over him when he remembered the erotic, yet violent, dream he had the previous week. "Yes, I'm fine, just a little under the weather. You kids carry every germ known to man."

Brenda smiled, but it was pained, almost identical to the prostitute's. "Oh, that's good." She was staring right at him. "My grandfather—" she stopped. "He was sick some years ago, like, *really* sick." Brenda paused, as if not knowing how to proceed. "I just…I was just checking. Sorry for being nosy." Her face became flushed, giving her cheeks a lovely rose shade—just like Ola's.

"Well, I appreciate your concern," Josef said. He knew she didn't believe him. It didn't take a doctor to tell something was wrong. Even the other staff, some of whom were nearly his age, had mentioned it. "But I'm just fine. I'm a tough old bird, you'll see. I'll bounce back in a few days. Don't think you'll get out of my test if I fall down dead." He knew the joke was distasteful as soon as it left his lips.

Brenda forced another smile and looked as a crowd of kids called her name.

Josef nodded to them. "Go on; it's Friday night. There's no need to be chatting with an old timer."

"Feel better, Mr. Lazer," she said, blending into the crowd.

Josef watched her walk away.

The gravity she possessed was strong, everyone flocked to her. She did her best to listen to them out of respect, but she slowed and turned, locking eyes with him again.

He shuddered. A chill ran through his body as if someone walked over his grave.

CHAPTER 13

Josef's car sat dark under a dead streetlight. He hadn't smoked in a while, but felt the occasion called for a pack of cancer sticks. What was the worst that could happen?

It wasn't as late as the last time he'd driven down to The Myers, so he wasn't sure if she'd be there. As he took a lap around Chamber Street, part of him wished she wouldn't be there, that she'd taken the night off, but he saw her. He knew it had to be her; none of the other girls had the softness like she did. She'd felt some kind of hurt in her life, something that gave her sympathy for Josef.

When he saw her leaning against a brick wall, his heart dropped. It was like seeing the doctor walk in with a metal tray containing a vaccine: you knew it was for the better, but it still didn't remove the fact it would hurt.

His nerves left him in a hurry when he drove by her. Their eyes locked and for a brief second, one of recognition, she smiled.

Josef hit the gas, driving away. When he was far enough, he did a U-turn and killed his lights. There, he sat chain-smoking with a pile of butts growing beside his door.

A light rain fell from the sky and some girls went for cover. He didn't see *her* any longer as the rain obscured his vision. Josef hit his wipers, but she was gone. His arm got wet as the rain drifted in through the open window.

"Hey, are you lookin' for some company?" a sweet voice asked from alongside the car.

Josef jumped, feeling his heart skip a beat. He turned and was face to face with her. There was no turning back. If he took off, leaving her standing in the cold rain, he wouldn't get another chance. He didn't think his body was going to hold out much longer anyway.

"Um, yes, yes I am," Josef said.

She smiled and walked around to the passenger side.

Josef tossed his cigarette out of the window, letting it hiss in the rain. He rolled the window up as the rain fell harder.

She jumped into the passenger seat and put her hands in front of the vents. "Thanks." She rubbed her palms together. After a moment, she reluctantly pulled them away. "I'm Sonny." Her hair was in a loose ponytail and her eyes, which looked only a few years removed from playing with dolls and believing in Santa Claus, carried a dullness in them.

Josef didn't have an alias, nor did he think one would be necessary. "Josef." He extended his hand.

Sonny looked at the offered hand and squinted.

Josef wasn't well-versed in soliciting prostitutes.

They shook hands briefly, but in Sonny's world, time is money. "So, what can I do for you?" she asked. Sonny turned in the seat to better face him. Her breasts peeked out from under her top. The smooth flesh was pale and still moist from the rain. "I'll suck you off for a twenty, or if you're up to it, you can fuck me in the backseat. That's extra, but I'm sure we can work something out." She licked her lips.

Josef hoped the interior of the car was dark enough so she couldn't see him blush. He was no prude, but he hadn't felt a woman since Ola, and at his age, he didn't know if he could even perform if he wanted to. "Ah, well, I was hoping for something a little different."

Sonny raised her eyebrows. "Sorry, I don't do anal. It's just not something I'm really into."

Josef's cheeks turned the shade of an overripe tomato. "No, no, not that either. It's nothing sexual at all."

Sonny laughed. She rested her chin in her hand and shook her head slightly. "So, why are we sitting here? Look, I'm grateful to not be standing in the rain, but time is money."

There's still time to turn back, Josef thought. *Tell her it was all a misunderstanding, give her a twenty, and send her on her way.* His brain was tortured, thinking of his options. Josef knew there was only one actual option.

As if being controlled by another person, Josef spoke. "This might sound crazy, but would you have dinner with me?"

"Dinner?"

"Yeah, nothing too fancy, just a nice little dinner at my house." He forced a smile. "I can make a mean chicken cutlet."

"Ahm, I don't go with johns to their houses. Sorry," Sonny said.

Josef nodded. Tears burned his eyes and made him sniffle. He thought he'd have to fake them, but they were real. "I'm sorry." He fished a handkerchief from his back pocket and wiped his eyes and nose. "My anniversary is coming up soon. It's the first one without my wife. I… I just didn't want to be alone." It pained him to watch her melt under his lie.

Sonny tilted her head and sighed, exhaling sympathy. "Well, I gue—"

"I'll pay," Josef blurted. "Five hundred for maybe two hours of your time, plus a hot meal. I'll even drive you back here, or wherever you'd like." Josef hoped he wasn't being too forward. A woman like Sonny probably had street smarts and if she smelled a trap, she'd never agree to go.

The sky opened up, and a bolt of lightning shot across the gloom, lighting up the grungy street. It was as if God was on his side. But if God was with *him*, who was with Sonny?

Sonny looked at the pouring rain and filth floating down the gutter. "Okay, it's a date." She gave a sincere smile.

Josef's heart broke for her, but he put the car in drive and, together, they entered the storm.

CHAPTER 14

The rain was steady and the wind increased. It took Josef longer to get home than he'd expected. Normally, he wouldn't have cared, but the fiery snake burrowed deep in his gut had other plans.

Josef and Sonny ran into the house and hung up their coats, and for the first time, he got a good look at her.

The young prostitute wasn't a spitting image of Brenda or Ola, but the features were there. She was a bit more weathered than the co-ed in his class, but the spirit of youth was still with her. She hadn't been completely broken yet.

Josef led her into the kitchen.

A bolt of pain tore into his stomach. Luckily, he'd been able to quell the pain on the drive over, but since he was standing and moving, his body had other plans. Sweat broke out on his brow, and his armpits and groin moistened. "If you'll excuse me a second," Josef said, as he pulled out a chair for the girl.

Sonny looked at him and could see the obvious pain on his face. "Sure." She sat as Josef shuffled out of the room.

He slammed the bathroom door. His arthritic fingers grappled with his pants. It was a losing battle and the only thing he could think of was the cold, damp shit stuck to his body when he'd lost his bowels in his bed. With only moments to spare, Josef's damp behind hit the cold toilet seat. Filth and blood came out of him like a geyser as tears fell down his cheeks.

Josef put his head in his hands and wept. "I can't fucking do it." Another cramp tore through his innards. More tears fell, some from the pain, but most from the decision he had to make. "Fuck!" He muffled his shout with his hand, then cleaned himself and wiped his face.

"Are you okay?" Sonny asked as he returned to the kitchen.

Josef knew he looked like hell; there was no point in lying to her, at least, completely. "No, I'm not." He opened the cupboard and removed a bottle of red wine and two glasses. With his back to her, he uncorked the bottle and poured. "I have cancer, Sonny. Stage four, the doctor said." Josef pulled a small piece of paper from his shirt pocket and dumped the crushed pill into her drink, hoping she didn't notice. Doctor Gosko said to be careful with them; they were strong. He hoped so.

"Oh my God, that's terrible," Sonny said. "Is there a cure or some treatment?"

Oh, there is, my girl. There's a cure, but not one that you're going to like, he thought. "I could've done chemo," he said, still swirling her wine glass. He didn't know how long he could keep his back to her before she grew suspicious. "But even that would only prolong the inevitable." He turned to her hoping the powder was gone. "I'd rather do things on my terms."

Sonny took the glass offered to her.

160

"I expect this to be my last anniversary, and then I can be with my family."

Sonny looked at him with the glass in her hand. A thin mist of tears shone in her clear eyes. She raised her glass. "To you."

Josef smiled and returned the toast, touching the rim of his glass to hers. "Thank you." He thought he was going to have a heart attack.

Sonny moved the glass towards her lips and slowed as if she saw something. If she spotted a piece of the pill, he'd be done for. All the trust he gained would be gone and she'd run from the house. There was no way, especially in his state, he could overpower her. That would be it. Josef would die, and the fate of Belphegor would be left to chance.

Sonny put the glass to her lips and drank. It wasn't a sip or a polite taste; it was a gulp, draining half the glass. She puckered her lips and smacked them a few times. "Mmm, that's pretty good."

Josef could've cried. Relief and fear washed over him. He sipped his wine, which tasted like vinegar in his mouth. "I'm glad you like it." He put his glass down and refilled hers.

Sonny drank again. She blinked. "Whoa, I'd better slow down." She stifled a burp with the back of her hand. "I'm already starting to feel this. Say, when are we eating? I need something to soak up this booze." Her eyelids drooped with lethargy.

"Another top-off?" Josef asked, holding the bottle.

Sonny didn't offer her glass, but she didn't say no as he poured. "You don't have to get me drunk to fuck me, you know that, right?" she asked with a smirk.

Josef smiled, but was far from happy. "I know, my dear. I know." He stood.

Sonny blinked again, this time slower.

"I just have to run downstairs to get the food, and then we can eat."

Sonny folded her arms on the table and rested her head on them. "Sure thing. I'm just gonna close my eyes for a minute." She picked her head up, her eyes finding his. There was just a hint of realization, of fear. "Hey, you didn't drug me, did you?"

"Shh, just close your eyes," Josef said as he headed into the basement.

CHAPTER 15

When Josef came back into the kitchen, Sonny was asleep. Low snores came from her nose, which rested on her arms.

"Sonny?" Josef asked, moving closer.

She didn't budge. Her breathing was strong, but consistent with sleep.

Josef touched her back, expecting her to jump, but still nothing. Gosko was right, the pills were strong. He hoped they were strong enough to keep her asleep through the next predicament: getting her, asleep, into the basement.

"Sonny." He rubbed her back, trying to get her to react. Josef picked up one of her arms and attempted to drape it around his neck. If he could get her to stand, he could guide her to the steps.

Nothing; she grumbled, but didn't move.

"Fuck." Josef pulled his neck from under her arm.

Sonny's balance shifted, sliding her slightly, and she tumbled to the kitchen floor. With a thump, her head hit the linoleum. Her eyelids fluttered as Josef grabbed an ankle.

He pulled her across the floor, his back screaming, but it was better than carrying her.

The maw of the basement lurked in front of him. He knew the horror awaiting them below. He could smell the corruption of the demon, the prince of Hell waiting to taste human flesh.

Josef took the first step down. He grabbed the railing with one hand and kept a firm grasp on Sonny's ankle with the other.

Sonny's head hit the stairs as Josef pulled. He winced and muttered an apology to the drugged woman. Doing his best to keep his balance, Josef pulled again.

Thump.

Thump.

Thump.

The sound of her skull skipping off the wood was like that of a heartbeat, as if the house's heart was racing, knowing what atrocity was about to be committed.

"Hmm," Sonny grumbled.

Josef, who'd been watching his step, not the woman, turned.

Sonny was waking up. Her eyelids fluttered as if waking from a dream. "Wha…what's going on?" Her eyes were cracked, but she couldn't see yet.

With a final yank, Sonny's head hit the concrete floor.

"Ah, you've done well, Pet Jew," Belphegor growled.

The putrid demon stood in the protective circle. His cracked horns looked like driftwood that had washed up on the banks of the river Styx. Open sores wept fluids every shade of rot. Each drop had a different viscosity, coating the beast's hellish flesh in a vile slickness. Belphegor's penis hung heavy and low. His glans was wrapped tight in a cocoon of taut foreskin. A centipede the size of a pencil skittered from the demon's urethra. The sharp legs dug into his meaty scrotum, leaving rents in the flesh. Belphegor was crouched low. His mouth, full of rows of jagged, cracked, and rotten teeth, was open, as if tasting the air.

"I haven't tasted cunt meat in a long time," the demon grumbled. He smiled. Thick drool ran from the corners of his mouth. "There's nothing like the taste of scared girl. Your reward will be great, Pet Jew." He sniffed the air like a foul dog. "She smells of fucking. I didn't think your old cock could do anything besides dribble piss. I will give her a true experience, a torment her cunt will never forget."

Josef recoiled at the sight of the demon. He couldn't help but look at the swelling penis rising between Belphegor's legs. "Just do it quick, please." he said. He pulled Sonny towards the circle, but she was stuck.

"No," Sonny grunted. Her chipped nails clung to the last step, holding on as if her life depended on it, and it did. Her drug-addled eyes were locked on the demon. With every passing second, the adrenaline in her body forced more of the drug out of her system.

Josef felt his grip weakening. A shock of pain ran through his stomach. He tried to adjust his hold on the girl, but she was thrashing.

"No!" Sonny screamed. The fight in her doubled. She kicked at Josef, breaking his grasp completely and striking his shin. With everything she had, Sonny tried to rush up the stairs, but the drug still had a hold on her. Her feet reacted like those of a newborn deer, causing her to sprawl on the bottom step.

Josef saw his life ending. Not only would he die, but his final days would be spent in a cold prison cell. There was no chance he could fight Sonny, and each moment she became stronger.

Sonny sprung to her wobbly feet and grabbed the railing. With a lurch, she started up the steps.

Josef reached for her. His fingers grazed the back of her heel, smacking her right foot into her left.

Sonny lost her balance. It was a slight tap, but more than enough to trip her up. She fell and smashed her chin on the stairs.

Taking the opportunity, Josef pounced on her, but there was no need to rush.

The prostitute was knocked out. Blood ran from her open mouth and a piece of her tongue was missing.

Josef used every ounce of strength he had to toss her back down the stairs.

Sonny tumbled to the concrete floor with Josef right behind her.

"Give her to me," Belphegor growled. "Push her into my Hell so I may taste her."

Josef couldn't allow Sonny to wake up again. He pulled and yanked, inching her closer to the protective circle. In his haste, Josef nearly crossed the threshold himself.

He stopped.

Was that the way out of it all? Just give himself to the demon and being done with fighting. No, he couldn't do that. It was unthinkable.

Sonny's eyes fluttered. Blood dribbled from her mouth as she screamed.

Josef pushed her leg through the barrier and into the grasp of Belphegor.

"Ah, yes, yes! Bitch meat!" Belphegor grabbed Sonny's leg, yanking her forward. He picked her up, making her stand facing away from him.

Josef and Sonny locked eyes. Hatred seethed from her glare as she screamed. It was something he had seen before—in his eyes' reflection when thinking of Kollmer. Instead, he was the monster now, not the Nazi lieutenant.

Belphegor sniffed at Sonny. "You didn't fuck her, did you?"

Josef didn't answer. His eyes stung, and he looked away from the scalding glare of Sonny.

"Let me show you what you missed," Belphegor said. His claws ripped through Sonny's clothes and flesh, leaving her nude, bleeding, and screaming. Sharp talons tore her skin and clothing into bloody strips.

Josef stared at her violated nudity.

One breast had been ripped almost clean off, dangling by clumps of fat. Her vagina was covered in short, dark pubic hair.

Belphegor held her by the throat with one hand. With the other, he ran a claw over her slit.

Sonny gasped at the violation of her body.

Belphegor removed his digit from her and put it in his mouth. "Ah, delicious. But it needs more blood." He released her throat and reached down to her vagina with both hands. Without hesitation, he thrust both claws into Sonny's opening.

She screamed as her flesh tore. Gore rushed from her sex as the demon opened her.

"No!" Josef yelled. His legs weakened, and he collapsed on the dirty basement floor.

Belphegor's hands were completely inside of her. He stared at Josef and pulled. Her vagina tore as he split her in half. Pelvis bones cracked with the pop of a pine knot in a fire. Fissures opened on her white belly. Fat peeked out, exposed to the light. Ripping and tearing, Belphegor split her further.

Entrails spilled from her, hitting the ground with a wet plop. The light faded from her eyes, but the violation of her body was far from over.

Belphegor grunted as Sonny's ribs broke in two. His mouth opened wide and bit her head off. He spat the mutilated skull at the barrier.

Josef flinched as it hit and fell to the ground. Sonny's left eye was ruptured, but the right was intact, staring at him with hatred. It was deserved.

With a final yell of exertion, Belphegor tore her corpse in half, splattering the barrier with undigested wine. He put half of Sonny's mangled vagina into his mouth and bit. Her flesh came off with a wet tear. "More cunt meat. I'll make you live forever." He swallowed and bit again. Ichor and slime ran from his maw.

Josef didn't know if he was going to shit or puke, but his stomach was a battlefield. He staggered up and grabbed the holy water.

The demon looked at him. Filth dripped from the hell-born body as Belphegor ripped more of Sonny to pieces. "One day, you will be mine, all mine, and then we will have some fun."

With tears in his eyes, Josef threw the holy water onto the demon, banishing him back into the stone.

CHAPTER 16

Three days later, Josef sat on his bed with a shotgun in his mouth. In front of him were pictures of Ola and the boys. He wanted them to be the last things he saw before he ended his miserable, murderous life.

After banishing Belphegor, Josef laid on the basement floor and wept. His tears stained the concrete, but the pain in his guts fled almost immediately. He cried not only out of remorse for taking an innocent life, but because he knew it was the right thing to do. Killing Sonny was the worst thing Josef had ever done, but it was necessary, an evil deed, but one he knew was for the better.

Though it was only three days since he'd killed Sonny, Josef felt twenty years younger. The pain in his stomach was gone and his appetite came back with a vengeance. Even after watching the poor girl be devoured, Josef couldn't stop himself from gorging on whatever he had in the house. He ate almost as much as he'd eaten when he was liberated from Auschwitz.

He called out sick from work, not knowing how'd he feel seeing familiar faces again. Sleeping was another concern of his. Every time he closed his eyes, he saw Sonny and the look on her face of betrayal, rage, and fear. It was always the fear that ripped Josef out of his fitful slumber. The look of knowing death was coming was something he'd seen on the faces of hundreds of death camp prisoners. It was a look he knew was probably plastered on the faces of his dead wife and sons before they were murdered.

On the second night after making the sacrifice, Josef decided it wasn't worth it. He knew his death would come eventually. The guilt and the shame of killing Sonny was too much.

On the morning of the third day, after eating a half dozen eggs, and a pound of bacon, Josef bought the shotgun. It was a burly gun, sporting twin barrels. He knew little about firearms, but he told the man behind the counter he'd be shooting something large. He bought a box of buckshot along with his gun. If he didn't think it would raise a red flag, he would've only asked for two shells, but the last thing he wanted was to arouse suspicion.

Each and every vehicle that drove by his house had Josef on edge. He didn't think anyone had seen Sonny get into his car on that rainy night, but the paranoia was still there. Part of him wanted to get caught. He didn't know why; maybe it was the guilt or the never-ending fear of being caught. It was the feeling of the ghettos all over again—knowing it wasn't going to end well, but waiting for the inevitable.

No cops came, and Josef knew they wouldn't. Even if someone had seen her get in his car, she'd never be found. Belphegor wouldn't allow that.

FOR THE BETTER

The third night, Josef laid out the pictures of his wife and kids, drank half a bottle of expensive bourbon, and loaded the gun.

Gun oil and metal were pungent on his tongue. Tears ran down his cheeks as he stared at the family he couldn't save, at the looks of shame on their faces, even though the pictures were decades old and faded. He wished he could tell them how sorry he was, how he regretted letting them be separated that day on the platform. If he'd known what would become of them, he would've forced the Nazis to kill them then and there; at least they could've died as a family.

Sobs racked Josef's body, causing the muzzle of the gun to dig into the roof of his mouth. His arm stretched towards the dual triggers of the shotgun. One blast would be more than enough to kill him, but Josef didn't want to leave anything to chance. His cold, quivering fingers found the smooth, curved triggers. Just a little bit of pressure…

Goodbye, he thought.

…the triggers didn't budge.

The safety!

Josef pushed the gun out of his mouth and threw it on the floor like it was a snake. Hot vomit rose in his throat, barely stifled by his hand as he rushed to the bathroom.

Most of his puke made it into the toilet before he collapsed. The cold tile welcomed him. It chilled the sweat on his flesh. He cried. "Never again. Never fucking again! Do you hear me? I'm done with you.

If I must die, I will, but I will never give you another life again." Josef punched the floor. The pain shot through his arm, but it felt good. It let him know he was still alive.

Josef wallowed in pain, both mental and physical. He made a deal at that moment, a pact that he'd never use the corrupt power of Belphegor again. If only he had the strength to keep it.

FOR THE BETTER

1ˢᵗ, May 2019

My 119ᵗʰ birthday has come and gone, and my life is finally ending. The cancer that I'd taken care of all those years ago—the same cancer I made my final human sacrifice for—is back. And it's back with a vengeance. My doctor told me I don't have long, and I believe him. I can feel it deep inside of me, wriggling in my bowels. Blood is the only thing that comes out of me. That and pain.

When I first knew the cancer was back, I was scared. Not of death. I think at this point I've made that abundantly clear. My soul is damned. That is a fact I made peace with decades ago. Whether it was lost in the camps when I did what needed to be done to survive, or if it was my first human sacrifice, I know I'm damned to Hell—a place I know all too well exists. And I know what beasts await me.

He is the reason I've always feared death. What would happen to the demon, Belphegor when I died? Sadly, I have the answer.

Many months ago, I befriended a young man named Robert. He is a good man, a hard worker, whose mother has the same dreaded disease as I. She is all the boy has in this world. They are each other's rocks, but her resolve is eroding. I can see it on his face when we speak. The bags under his eyes, the lethargy, and the long gazes at nothing. I have seen grief and he and I are very well acquainted. But Robert is my only hope. He's the only one who may be able to keep the secret of the demon, and who may be able to use the power of the beast for good. It is an evil burden I'm considering, but what else am I to do? I cannot rid myself of this rock; it is mine to bear.

I do not know how to approach the subject with him, but I know it must be soon. The cancer is eating me alive. I feel like I'm made of dry paper and a flame is torching me. Days, but probably hours, are all that remain in my life. Getting this close to the finish line, to handing the burden off only to die mere moments before would be a cruel fate. Something I deserve, undoubtedly. I cannot allow that to happen.

Over twenty years ago, on the bathroom floor with a mouth full of sick, I made a pact that I would no longer use the power of evil. But I cannot let evil win. The only way I can survive and have enough strength to see this through is another sacrifice. It can't be a human. No one knows me, and there's not enough strength left in my old bones to drag a person down the steps. So, it has to be a dog. My life has been full of them, from the killers that ripped Abe apart, to my beloved Schatzi, dogs have always been there.

It pains me to do it, but tomorrow I will go to the shelter. I just hope I have enough time.

FOR THE BETTER

My Final Entry

Her name was Molly.

I don't know why I wrote that, but it seems only fair to the old gal to be remembered. She doesn't know what she's done for me, for the world. But, the one thing I know for sure is that I'll never get the sound of her screams out of my mind.

My time has finally come. I wish I could scrawl something heroic, claiming I wasn't scared, but I'm fucking terrified. Those people who claim they don't fear death are liars. Everyone fears the unknown, even if it is taking them away from the pains of the flesh. Day in and day out, I watched my fellow prisoners walk around with that look on their faces. And when they'd become lax, one of them would catch a bullet in the back of the head—or worse.

Robert will be here soon. He trusts me. He likes me and I like him. But I can't help but feel like a monster. Leaving this burden on a man with so much heartache in his life. It was not a decision easily made, but there is no other choice.

I'm sitting at my kitchen table. A table I never shared a meal with my family at. But they are with me. Spread out amongst pictures of atrocities are pictures of them. My family. A reminder to me of why I fought. Why I still fight.

It's getting late and Robert will be here soon. This book, like all of my secrets, will die with me. It is not meant for anyone's eyes but mine. Before I go and accept my fate, I wish to make peace. A final declaration, if you would.

To Ola- I love you more today than I did the day I first laid eyes on you. You were the best thing in my life, a true God-send. But, I'm sorry, my love. Your husband has not been a good man. He has done things—horrid things—in the name of survival. Things I thought would help, that deep in the back of my mind I knew were for the better. If I could've seen what I would become, I would've gladly died in those camps with you and our boys.

To Michal and Piotr- My boys. My strong, brave boys. I hope you are safe and happy playing with your toys. I regret every moment I missed with you. Every punishment—no matter how small—that I ever doled out to you. I miss your laughs and our jokes. Boys, I am so sorry. I am your father, your protector, and I have failed you. My death will come not knowing the torments you faced in the hands of monsters, and for that I'm grateful. Please, watch over your mother, for I know that I cannot.

And to Robert- I'm sorry for what I've left to you.

God forgive me.

ABOUT THE AUTHOR

Daniel J. Volpe is the splatterpunk award-winning author of PLASTIC MONSTERS. His love for horror started at a young age when his grandfather unwittingly rented him "A Nightmare on Elm Street." Daniel has published with D&T Publishing, Potter's Grove, The Evil Cookie Publishing, and self published. He can be found on Facebook @ Daniel Volpe, Instagram @ dj_volpe_horror and Twitter @DJVolpeHorror Signed books can be found at djvhorror.com

Printed in Great Britain
by Amazon